All Write!

Northern England
Edited by Allison Dowse

Disclaimer

Young Writers has maintained every effort
to publish stories that will not cause offence.

Any stories, events or activities relating to individuals
should be read as fictional pieces and not construed
as real-life character portrayal.

First published in Great Britain in 2004 by:
Young Writers
Remus House
Coltsfoot Drive
Peterborough
PE2 9JX
Telephone: 01733 890066
Website: www.youngwriters.co.uk

All Rights Reserved

© *Copyright Contributors 2004*

SB ISBN 1 84460 629 5

Foreword

Young Writers was established in 1991 and has been passionately devoted to the promotion of reading and writing in children and young adults ever since. The quest continues today. *Young Writers* remains as committed to engendering the fostering of burgeoning poetic and literary talent as ever.

This year, *Young Writers* are happy to present a dynamic and entertaining new selection of the best creative writing from a talented and diverse cross-section of some of the most accomplished primary school writers around. Entrants were presented with three inspirational and challenging themes.

'Mini Sagas' set pupils the challenge of writing a story in 50 words or less. This style of story telling required considerable thought and effort to create a complete story with such a strict word limit.

'A Day In The Life Of . . .' offered pupils the chance to depict twenty-four hours in the lives of literally anyone they could imagine. A hugely imaginative wealth of entries were received encompassing days in the lives of everyone from the top media celebrities to historical figures like Henry VIII or a typical soldier from the First World War.

Finally 'Short Stories' offered the authors free reign with their writing style and subject matter. All themes encouraged the writer to open and explore their minds as they used their imagination to produce the following selection.

All Write! Northern England is ultimately a collection we feel sure you will love, featuring as it does the work of the best young authors writing today. We hope you enjoy the work included and will continue to return to *All Write! Northern England* time and time again in the years to come.

Contents

Barnard Castle CE Primary School, Co Durham
Elisabeth Harding (10)	1
Victoria Herbert (8)	2
Ellen Gilbert (8)	3
Jessica Trevett (9)	4
Jessica Lee-Shield (9)	5
Ann Longstaff (9)	6
Jenny Sparrow (8)	7
Scott Hunter (10)	8
Jack Holguin (8)	9
Robert Mounter (9)	10
Andrew Gold (8)	11
Marcus Sowerby	12
Rebecca Watson	13
Tom Herbert (9)	14
Amy Tones (9)	15
Jake Sowersby (7)	16
Bryony Gargett (8)	17
Emily Bonnett	18
Olivia Stevenson (8)	19
Alice Wood	20
Stacey Walker (8)	21
Fiona Cook (9)	22
Mary Moore (10)	23
Jade Hadden (10)	24
Kelsey-Jade Maughan (10)	25
Louise Lockwood (10)	26
Laura Hackett (10)	27
Eve Berry (10)	28
Emily Collings (10)	29
Josh Harper (10)	30

Broughton-in-Furness CE Primary School, Cumbria
India Ratcliffe (11)	31
Helen Satterthwaite (11)	32
Tom Winch (11)	33
Joshua Ratcliffe (11)	34
Diane Atkinson (11)	35
Hayley Robinson (11)	36

Emma Garnett (11)   37
Claudia Bland (11)   38

Cragside Primary School, Newcastle upon Tyne
Jacob Frame (11)   39
Bobbie-Faye Keelan (11)   40
Julian Wyton (11)   41
Neil Davies (11)   42
Jenna Ferguson (11)   43
Samuel Kennedy (11)   44
Connor Brown (11)   45
Ben Goldie (11)   46
Gabrielle Armstrong (10)   47
Conor Reichal (11)   48
Jonathan Snell (11)   49
Madeleine O'Hara (10)   50
Madeleine Macaulay (11)   51
Lauren Matthewson (11)   52
Louise Hollingsworth (11)   53
Chris Mole (11)   54
James Hedley (11)   55
Madoc Flynn (11)   56
Joshua Oliver (11)   57
Ashley Hildyard (11)   58
Nathan Harwood (11)   59
Andrew Watson (11)   60
Samantha McNally (11)   61
Rachel Darby (10)   62
Zak Hubbard (11)   63
Sarah-Jay Davidson (11)   64
Barney Wallace (11)   65
Ruby Catherall (11)   66
Farijan Begum Sufi (11)   67
Joe Withers (11)   68
Alex Fawcett (11)   69
Sarah Robinson (11)   70
Sarah Henderson (11)   71
Amy Louise Biwer (11)   72
Simon Anderson (11)   73
Lisa Waggett (11)   74
Christopher Richardson (11)   75

Andy Lee Robertson (11) — 76
Faye Armstrong (11) — 77
Kerry-Anne Eileen Browne (10) — 78
Matthew Phillips (11) — 79
Samantha Baker (11) — 80
Jake Fothergill (11) — 81

Greenland Junior School, Co Durham
Dominic Donkin (10) — 82
Emily Thynne (10) — 83
Rebekah West (10) — 84
Jamie Caisley (10) — 85
Alex Jobson (10) — 86
Roshni Miah (10) — 87
Amy Halliday (10) — 88
Jade Sutton (10) — 89
Tamara Brown (10) — 90
Laura Ridley (10) — 91
Ryan Purvis (10) — 92
Christopher Graham (9) — 93

Holy Cross RC Primary School, North Tyneside
Michael Hilton (11) — 94

Hunwick Primary School, Co Durham
Sally Grace Pentecost (9) — 95
Laura Bradshaw (8) — 96
Jack Liddell (9) — 97
Christopher Housecroft (10) — 98
Megan Maddison (9) — 99
Nicole Green (10) — 100
Richard James (9) — 101
Jamie Campbell (9) — 102
Ellie Pryce (10) — 103

Kelloe Primary School, Co Durham
Amy Jury (11) — 104
Rosie Craggs (11) — 105
Laura Williams (10) — 106
Emma Turton (10) — 107

Colin Hall (11)	108
Shannon Richardson (11)	109
Samantha Dobson (11)	110
Daley Hetherington (11)	111
Carl Hill (11)	112
Matthew Daley (11)	113
Jessica Taylor (9)	114
Bethany Morrow (9)	115
Nicola Potts (10)	116
Robert Crawford (10)	117
Liam Simpson (10)	118
Laura Jones (9)	119
Ruby Finley (9)	120
Cara Thompson (9)	121
Allan Jordan (10)	122
Philip Jones (10)	123
Jade Templeton (10)	124
Samantha Hill (9)	125

Langwathby CE Primary School, Cumbria

Edward Kidd (8)	126
Cameron Harvey (8)	127
Bradley Neen (9)	128
James Sharp (9)	129
Lauren Snowball (9)	130
Megan Wilson (9)	131
Isobel Everatt (8)	132
Tom Holme (8)	133
Harry Leah (8)	134
Donald Burrow (9)	135
Holly Streatfield (8)	136
Ellen Greenop (8)	137
Megan Liddle (8)	138
Alice Sandells (8)	139
Rebecca Didcock (8)	140
Jonathan Crisp (8)	141

St Mary's Meadowside Primary School, Sunderland

Aiden Goulden (10)	142
Christie Bainbridge (10)	143
William Lewis (9)	144

Melanie Golding (10)	145
Ashleigh Simpson (10)	146
Matthew Wake (10)	147
Caitlin Hindmarsh (9)	148
Georgina Currie (10)	149
Emily Bird (10)	150
Jessica Pye (10)	151
Sarah Forrest (10)	152
Rebecca Smith (10)	153
Anthony Callaghan (10)	154
Luke Gibbins (10)	155
Katherine Lamb (10)	156
Craig MacDonald (10)	157
Melissa Quinn (10)	158
Eszter Soos (10)	159
Mark Middleton (10)	160
Daniel Pinchen (10)	161
Josie Barlow (10)	162
Paige Gilbert (10)	163
Olivia Newby (10)	164
Cameron Phillips (10)	165

St Mary's RC Primary School, Newcastle upon Tyne
Elliot Harris (9)	166
Beth Wilkinson (9)	167
Mairead Hunt (9)	168
Rachael Bell (11)	169
Stephanie Saxelby (9)	170
Calum Sordy (9)	171
Isabella Mercer Jones (8)	172
Daragh Rogerson (9)	173
Jack Thompson (9)	174
Emily Norman (9)	175
Sarah Boyd (9)	176

Shincliffe CE Primary School, Co Durham
Daniel Tiffin (8)	177
Emma Farman (8)	178
Louise Carnaby (8)	179
Lucy Kirkup (8)	180
Oliver Hobson (7)	181

Robert Blalek (8) 182
Elliot Kay (8) 183
Felix Dayan (7) 184
Ewan Hill (8) 185
Alison Laing (8) 186
Emma Callaghan (8) 187
Olivia Karnacz (8) 188
Gemma Morgan (8) 189
Rebecca Lambert (8) 190
Mae Cuthbertson (7) 191
Jason Jones (8) 192
David Mitchell (8) 193
Kate Wood (8) 194
Gabrielle Latcham (8) 195

Swalwell Primary School, Newcastle upon Tyne
Nathan Finlay (10) 196
James Gillender (10) 197
Gary Boyd (11) 198
Vanessa Pears (9) 199
David McGee (11) 200
Shaun Kavanagh (11) 201
Leighton Wright (11) 202
Steven Clark (11) 203
Danny Summerside (11) 204
Connor Mullins (10) 205
Shannon White (9) 206
James Wilson (11) 207
Chloe Halliday (11) 208
Ashley Turner (11) 209
Adam Watson (10) 210
Jade Urwin (9) 211
Michael Hall (10) 212

The Creative Writing

A Day In The Life Of Queen Elizabeth II

A butler came through the large oak doors, followed by Prince Charles.
'Prince Charles, Your Royal Highness,' came the butler's ringing voice.
   Prince Charles walked in, his head held high, his nose basically facing the ceiling.
   'You are the next one to be on the throne. Take it in pride and honour. You are dismissed.'
   Prince Charles nodded and walked out of the room.

Elisabeth Harding (10)
Barnard Castle CE Primary School, Co Durham

A Day In The Life Of A Nurse

My name is Gemma Scott and I work in Bishop Auckland Hospital. Last night was the worst night ever. We had a patient who had brain damage from falling down the stairs. There were people everywhere rushing about and shouting.

We put her in a hospital bed and examined her. I had just walked in the room when everyone had found out she was very badly hurt. Her husband was very upset when he had found out so he had to sit in the café with another nurse. The only way to help her was to give her an operation in the operating theatre. We also had to make sure that she could talk fine and understand what we were saying.

We did some little tests on her to make sure she was definitely OK. When we had finished she could talk and understand what we were saying quite well.

We thought everything would be fine after we had finished operating on her and everything else. All the people that I was working with were very pleased because we had helped her.

Victoria Herbert (8)
Barnard Castle CE Primary School, Co Durham

A Day In The Life Of Lord Nelson

Yells and cries of men on deck, the sound of gunshots filled the air. It is I, Lord Horatio Nelson, captain of HMS Victory.

I put on my hat and coat and ran on the top deck. Ships from Spain and France were beside us.

Bang! Went the cannon, a French ship was damaged. I looked on one of the ships and there stood Napoleon Bonaparte, France's general was commanding their ship. Men were lying on deck and I was wondering if we would win.

After a long battle Napoleon was defeated. I felt proud with myself and the crew from HMS Victory for beating the French.

Ellen Gilbert (8)
Barnard Castle CE Primary School, Co Durham

A Day In The Life Of A Monk

It was 3am on a cold winter's morning. All the boys at Egglestone Abbey were huddled round the warmth of the fire. All we had to wear was a thin little robe and to make things worse our heads were shaved! I started to think of God with all his splendour on high. But my daydream was broken by the sound of the chore bell. My morning task was to milk all five cows. By the time I had finished I was exhausted. But I had to wait another hour before breakfast meanwhile having morning prayers.

The Latin was hard and my throat was sore from so many prayers. In the middle of the service I needed to go so I was quite relieved when we were told to go to our dormitories (in Latin of course!).

At breakfast I ate ravenously and I was so hungry I got caught stealing holy bread for the evening service! As a punishment I was sent to Gospel writing, three hours of painful writing. I was just thinking how to abandon my mind when the blessed lunch bell rang.

I wished it wasn't so cold. I sat, shivering on St John's stone benches. It was yet another service. The abbot droned on until I thought he must be quite out of breath! Then at last it was glorious tea. This time I didn't steal any food. By the end of tea I was exhausted. The abbot saw me yawn and made me go to bed early and I was glad of it. For I knew another day of hard work was coming up tomorrow!

Jessica Trevett (9)
Barnard Castle CE Primary School, Co Durham

A Day In The Life Of PC Polly Page

I have just finished my shift of being a policewoman. I am glad the day has finished. There was an awful case today. I was working with PC Cathy Bradford, one of my colleagues. We had just stopped for a drink while we waited for a case to attend to. We were stood in the queue to Sally's Handy Snacks which was parked in the lay-by next to the reservoir. In front of us in the queue there was an old man who had left his grandchildren in the car while he ordered what looked like a lolly and drink for them both. His grandchildren were in the car with the keys in. I knew something was going to happen. The children were screaming and giggling in the car, they were climbing around the front seats like two little babies. In the background the reservoir was swishing and swaying with the strong force of the breeze.

When the man went back to the car the children had locked the doors and keys were still in. I stood and watched him mouth through the window to open the doors, evidently I could see they weren't going to listen but let him have another go.

'Polly! Polly!' Cathy was shouting in my ear. 'What do you want?'

'Oh I'll just have some lemonade,' I replied. When I turned around I saw their grandad stood with the lollies and the drinks then the car started to sink into the reservoir!

I called the fire brigade and the ambulance, they came but could not help us. The car sank fully. An ambulance driver then dived. He came out with only the girl.

A couple of weeks later the boy's body was found, sadly dead.

Jessica Lee-Shield (9)
Barnard Castle CE Primary School, Co Durham

A Day In The Life Of Florence Nightingale

Hello and nice to meet you, I am Florence Nightingale. It is 1854 and the Crimean War has begun.

I wanted to be a nurse so I went to an army camp to nurse the men in the Crimean War. They didn't want me to be a nurse even though they needed more help. The hospital was dirty and smelt, the toilets were flooded and there were rats and mice everywhere. The soldiers were in pain and weren't getting much help. I eventually got them to let me help. That day I told everybody to start scrubbing the floors and to clean the hospital. After a few hours the hospital was looking clean. They kept on washing the hospital. By nine o'clock the hospital was the cleanest hospital around.

That night I was on watch with my lamp, that is how I've become known as the 'lady with the lamp'. At about half-past ten there was a huge gunshot.

A few hours later when I was still on watch, a man rushed in with a stretcher. On it was a man holding his arm in agony. We did as much as we could and after hours of trying we finally got the man back to normal. He stayed overnight but went back to fight the next day. After that man I went to sleep till the next morning.

Goodbye!

Ann Longstaff (9)
Barnard Castle CE Primary School, Co Durham

A Day In The Life Of Willy Wonka

Hi, I'm Willy Wonka. Last week some children came to visit the factory. Now I don't normally let people into the factory but I felt it was time for someone else to run the factory. I didn't want a grown-up to run it so I decided to have a sensible child run it instead. The children who bought a chocolate bar with a golden ticket in would be able to come into the factory. The child that lasted the longest in the factory would win.

When the children got to the gates of the factory they were taken inside by me. When we got inside I took them straight to the chocolate waterfall. Three of the children wanted to swim in the chocolate water. I told them not to but they jumped straight in. They didn't realise how deep it was and drowned. That only left Charlie and Amy. Amy's best friend had jumped into the water so Amy (being daft as a brush) jumped in after her. That only left Charlie. Charlie was the winner!

Jenny Sparrow (8)
Barnard Castle CE Primary School, Co Durham

A Day In The Life Of Thierry Henry

The morning began when my alarm clock went off at half-past nine. I always get up early to start training. I have to have my cereal and get kitted up for footie. The boss called me and said, 'Get to the football stadium and start training for a friendly match against Man U on Monday.'

As soon as I found out I went straight to the football stadium, all my other teammates were there, such as Jens Lehmann, Ashley Cole, Sol Campbell, Toure, Lauren, Pires, Vieira, Edu, Ljungberg and Reyes. The last time I saw them was in the FA Cup, it is good to be back with all my teammates again.

Scott Hunter (10)
Barnard Castle CE Primary School, Co Durham

A Day In The Life Of Aragorn From Lord Of The Rings

Ah, this is the story of the last battle I fought to protect Gondor at Mideasus Thurt (it's a battlefield).

I, Aragorn was sitting at the throne of Gondor with my wife Arwen (as usual), discussing the type of things politicians discuss, when the horn of Gondor went off. I rushed out the throne room summoning the armies of Gondor, the bowmen (archers), horsemen (cavalry), swordsmen (warriors) of Gondor and I leapt onto Begow (my horse).

My armies of Gondor and I rode proudly into battle and went forwards into a stampede with the Black Riders swooping down, and the Orcs!

The Rohan cavalry came 1,000,000 of them! This was just 2 years ago from now. After hours of war we won, but many were killed.

Jack Holguin (8)
Barnard Castle CE Primary School, Co Durham

A Day In The Life Of PC Plum

One day I woke up and went downstairs because the phone was ringing. It was my boss, he wanted me to go on nightshift.

'OK then,' I replied and went off to watch TV.

Then Billy and Jonny came down, my two sons. That was the end of my peace and quiet. I just about made it through the day with Billy and Jonny.

At 5.30 I got ready to go to the police station. I got there and saw that Phil, Carl and Bob were on nightshift as well.

At 8 o'clock I got a call about 5 men smashing a jewellery shop window and nicking the world's biggest diamond, so I rushed out and got in the car and drove off to find them. In the distance I saw 5 or 6 men running away laughing. So I took the handbrake off and zoomed off.

Suddenly 2 cars came up the road. I hit the car and span round and round. The car hit the 5 men and they got arrested and the diamond was saved.

Robert Mounter (9)
Barnard Castle CE Primary School, Co Durham

A Day In The Life Of Wayne Rooney

Yesterday I went outside to see what the weather was like, it was hot. I needed to know because I was going to the football club. It was a nice day, I wondered if it would rain because then it would be cancelled.

I got my clothes on and set off. It was a long time but I still got there in the end.

Sven said, 'You're early.'

'Here comes Becks,' I said.

'Hello,' finally Nicky came.

'Now men, first we are doing corners, David you first, then you Rooney and then you Cole.'

'OK,' said Cole.

We finished. I was quick getting back as I was starving. I had chips, beans, sausages then had a bath and had milk, and went to bed, exhausted.

Andrew Gold (8)
Barnard Castle CE Primary School, Co Durham

A Day In The Life Of A WWII Soldier

Me and a crew of D-Day representatives were just about to abandon HMS Newcastle, when a large, bold atomic hit the ship's huge bow. There was an almighty bang and we all flew overboard a few metres from the Berlin shore. The water once a crystal-blue had turned rose-red and there were dead bodies everywhere! I'd never forget this dreadful, gory sight. But the worst was still to come, I told my shaking self I needed to fight for my king and country.

I paddled onto the beach and took cover in a shell hole. I pulled out my heavy Thompson machine gun, took careful aim, squeezed the trigger and started filling the German bunkers with lead but I knew I couldn't stay there for long, so I yelled at the top of my lungs, 'Covering fire!'

The noise started, the British Navy Seals threw a hail of bullets at the Germans and as fast as my legs would go I flew off down the coast and dived behind an old rusty WWI tank. Rapidly I got a bolder grenade out and lobbed it at the tank - *boom!* A side of the tank blew up, this was exactly what I wanted. I waddled inside and saw a rocket left in its turret. I feverishly turned the pointer to north and turned it at the barbed wire fence. *Boom!* The fence flew into a million pieces.

I hopped out and dived under the fence, the German machine guns started to fire. I ran up close to the bulletless bunker, I was getting shot at by the German gate guards, one 2-inch bullet just missed my right shoulder. I pulled out my Colt pistol and started picking them off. I ran up the tunnel trying to be as quiet as possible. I entered the bunker after having to silence another guard . . .

Marcus Sowerby
Barnard Castle CE Primary School, Co Durham

A Day In The Life Of An Air Hostess

It was September 19th and I was on a small plane with about five adults and only two babies, Carolynn and Michaela. They were all travelling to Cyprus. We were making our journey by flying over the Mediterranean Sea. The children were fast asleep, probably dreaming about the hot weather. The adults were happily playing a challenging game of Monopoly. Leah was the mum of Michaela and Carolynn and she was winning by ten thousand pounds. Jackline (one of the adults) was losing by loads.

Just then, I stopped pouring the Coke that Leah and all of her friends, Frank, Jackline, Rosie and Craig had ordered because the plane shuddered. All of the drinks spilt, the baby seat jerked forward and all of the counters flew off the Monopoly board and landed on one of the seats. Michaela and Carolynn awoke and started crying. Being a air hostess is amazing, going to different places and learning lots of unusual languages.

I tottered along to the pilot's cabin in my high heels and asked him what was happening.

He said, 'We've hit a mega electric storm because of the heat, but the plane can't take the power.' He continued, 'If the plane gets struck by lightning it will sink to the ocean's floor.'

There was no time to waste. I had to get everyone a life jacket and an inflatable dinghy, just in case we did fall into the sea.

Just then, the plane started to fall. I reached for the life jackets but they weren't there. Who'd taken them? All the pressure was on the pilot and me! But I couldn't find the jackets or dinghies.

Whoosh! The plane kept slamming down on the sea and rising. It made one last slam, but then, it started to sink. I tried to get everyone off the plane, but the babies' seats wouldn't come undone. The water was up to my chin. It was very awful, though it was warm.

Kerplink! The seat which Michaela was sat in, finally came undone. I struggled to hold on to her as I got Carolynn out. I gave the babies to Leah and Frank.

That was it! I'd moved the jackets to the shelf in the cabin! I collected them and swam safely to the people. We were safe. It took a day to be safe but it was worth it.

By a miracle the next day I was on a massive rescue boat. I will always remember that exciting but frightening day as an air hostess.

Rebecca Watson
Barnard Castle CE Primary School, Co Durham

A Day In The Life Of A Farmer

I got up at 5.30am. I put on some work clothes and went downstairs for my breakfast. I had a teacake and a cup of coffee. Then I put on my boiler suit.

As I got outside I smelt fire. I zoomed round the corner and saw my hay was on fire. I went stiff and froze. I ran around the corner and went to the phone and shouted, 'Fire! Fire! at the Black Boyde Farm, come qu- . . .' the line went dead.

When they got there I showed them where it was, so they went straight to work.

It took about half an hour to put the fire out. When they put all the pipes away I had to pay them. It was a lot of money because it was also a big fine. It cost a whopping 2 grand! As they left I got on with my work.

I had to feed the cows and bulls, the sheep and pigs and llamas with corn instead of hay!

Tom Herbert (9)
Barnard Castle CE Primary School, Co Durham

A Day In The Life Of A Policeman

One day PC John went to work. He had just sat down when the phone rang. He answered it and said, 'Hello, who is it?' He could hear noises in the background.
'Help! Help!' shouted a man.
'Where are you?' he shouted back.
'Yorkshire Bank.'

So off he went to Yorkshire Bank and saw a robber run out and down the Market Cross, so he put his car into 4th gear and darted round the corner and cars skidded out of the way. He crashed his car in the church car park, unbuckled his belt, unlocked his door, ran after the robber and caught him. He got all of the money and put a spray on the robber's hands to drop the rest of the money and got in the car. He put handcuffs on him and tried to find another policeman to help him take him back to the police station and to jail.

So he took him to jail and locked him up.

PC John went home and had his tea and watched TV and went to bed to rest ready for a whole new day tomorrow.

Amy Tones (9)
Barnard Castle CE Primary School, Co Durham

A Day In The Life Of A Policeman

One day a policeman was controlling the traffic when a van came flying down the road, and the policeman had to jump out the way!

The policeman jumped onto his motorbike, and went flying off to try and catch him. The van was going very fast indeed and the policeman found it very hard to catch it. The van was at full speed.

Finally the motorbike with the policeman on caught up with the van. The man in the van went faster so the policeman went faster. The policeman went in front of the van and got him pulled off the road. He took him to the police station.

The policeman looked in the back of the man's van. It was full of stolen stuff! The policeman was furious. He went in the van with the robber to put all the stuff back. The robber had to drive it because the policeman did not know where he got it all from. The problem was solved. The robber had to go back to the police station. The policeman wanted a word with the robber!

Jake Sowersby (7)
Barnard Castle CE Primary School, Co Durham

A Day In The Life Of A Policewoman

One day I was on my way to work and I got a call from the police station saying, 'Hurry up! I need you to investigate something.'

When I arrived at the police station I had to go to someone's house because there had been a robbery, it was in Barney, it was a sunny day so I did not mind doing jobs.

When I got to the house she told me that her favourite ornaments had been taken and £500. She was crying.

The next day I saw a teenager, he was a boy running out of Barney so I followed him, but kept a bit away from him, so he did not see me. He went well past the golf course then he stopped and jumped over a wall, into the field near someone's house. I stopped the car and parked on the side of the road. I looked over the wall and he had £500 and the ornaments. So I jumped over the wall and just caught him. I told him, 'I am afraid, I heard about the robbery and you have got the same stuff that was taken, you are under arrest.' So I took him to jail.

At the police station I asked him if he had taken anything else. He said no. I took the things off him and took them back to the owner.

When I got back to the police station the teenager was crying. I asked him what was wrong, he said he wanted to talk to his dad on the phone. I phoned his house, his dad answered. I explained he was in prison then I gave the phone to the boy, he said everything he wanted to say, he gave it back to me and then he went to sleep, feeling a bit better.

Bryony Gargett (8)
Barnard Castle CE Primary School, Co Durham

A Day In The Life Of A Builder

I puffed my cigarette, I looked up at the new block of flats. We had started in March 2001, now it was planned to be finished by December 2003. I thought it had gone up at a remarkable rate. It was 7 floors high. It would have 35 flats.

A twig fell down from one of the 17 oak trees that surrounded the site. It caught the end of my cigarette. The twig set on fire and fell down to the floor where there was lots of burnable materials. Soon there was a blazing fire by my feet. 'Fire!' I shouted. I emptied my water bottle on the fire, the rest of the team did the same. Nothing was going to work. The fire spread to the building.

A builder called Paul phoned the fire brigade. 'Away,' was all he said, then, 'phoned ones at Ricklton.'

I knew it would take them the best part of an hour to get here. I suddenly realised Matt was trapped in one of those rooms!

I hurriedly told the rest of the team. We got the ladder which was used to paint with. I placed a foot on the ladder, I had to do it! I climbed the ladder and looked through the window, I saw Matt, but there was no chance of getting in that window. I edged to the edge of the ladder. I hauled myself up onto the window sill. It was boiling, I went out of the door, it was only a hole. I went out onto the corridor, there was a line of ashes to show where the banisters had been. I gasped for breath. With a lot of tugging I opened the door to the room Matt was in. I saw Matt's face as white as a sheet. I was sure we were going to die, we both weren't fit enough to make the journey back.

I pulled my last bit of strength together and said, 'Stay here!'

We stayed there for ages. Eventually I heard the siren. They broke through the window and took Matt to hospital.

Emily Bonnett
Barnard Castle CE Primary School, Co Durham

A Day In The Life Of A Sailor

Yesterday Mr Macredeis was sailing across the sea to find and look at the blue whale. He had his breakfast before going on the search. As he ate his breakfast the boat banged against a rock. At that moment he knew he was on shore at Japan.

He did not know how to speak Japanese and he was lost, he looked in the food shops, there was nothing he fancied. His wife, Sally, was at home with his children so he bought her some jewellery, the youngest child a little magnetic set, the oldest one a doll that was hand-made and for himself he bought a footstool. There was lots of stuff and he thought it was time to have tea.

He had another look around. Finally he got some noodles and ate them. He set off again on his journey. He thought he should give up until something knocked the boat again, but this time the sea was too deep for it to be a rock and he was in the part where the blue whale lived. As it swam further away, the faster the boat went until he could see it, it was beautiful. He had to let it go so he did and had tea. He got home safely but there will be another adventure another day.

Olivia Stevenson (8)
Barnard Castle CE Primary School, Co Durham

A Day In The Life Of A Shop Assistant

One day there was a girl called Tanya who was walking to work. It was about 8am and she'd not long woken up. She was half asleep. She eventually arrived at work. One of her friends called Sophie was opening the tills. The customers were shouting, 'Come on, open this damn shop!'

'Just hang on, we'll open the doors when we are ready!'

So they waited and waited until the doors flung open. All of the customers rushed in and knocked Tanya over!

Nearly all of the customers had gone by now. It had just turned 12pm.

'I'm going for my lunch break now.'

'OK,' replied Sophie.

As she was leaving the desk in walked someone that looked funny and was wearing a footie top with 'Beckham' on the back. Tanya rushed back to the desk and asked, 'What would you like Sir?'

'I'm just wondering if you have any footballs?'

'Of course, follow me.' As Tanya walked out of the counter she nudged Sophie.

She started to walk up to the top of the shop. As she was walking up she didn't take her eyes off David because she loved him. When they got to the top of the shop Tanya started to look for the balls. 'Here you are.'

'Thanks.' As he took it out of her hands he touched her and she went and fell.

'Oh, what have I done to you?' he asked. He picked her up and carried her up to the desk. He put her down on the floor.

Sophie had sorted her out by lifting her up. Beckham was stood there.

Tanya said, 'Thanks for helping me.'

'It's OK,' and he gave her a kiss on the cheek.

It was time for Tanya to go home now.

When she arrived at home she told her mam what happened at work. She never would forget that day. When she looked in the newspaper she saw an article about what had happened on that fantastic day.

Alice Wood
Barnard Castle CE Primary School, Co Durham

A Day In The Life Of A Policeman

One day PC Jake, who was a policeman, got up for work when the alarm clock rang at seven o'clock.

He got dressed in his uniform and went downstairs for breakfast. It took him about ten minutes to eat his breakfast. After breakfast he sat down to watch a bit of the news.

'Oh no, it's half-past seven already, I have to go to work,' he said, very shocked. He put on his shoes and went to get the keys to lock the door. He locked the door and got in the car and drove to work quite quickly in case he was needed.

He was needed, as soon as he put his foot in the door he was called out.

He got to the Yorkshire Bank because there had been a robbery. He went into the bank, and as soon as he set foot in the door the robbers ran out.

'How much did they steal?' Jake asked.

'About a hundred pounds,' replied the banker.

No sooner had the banker said that, Jake ran out the door as fast as he could. He got down to the butter market before he caught them. He forced them to give back the money. It took about five minutes before they gave it back. He walked up and took the money back to the bank and took them to the station. He went out to the car park and got in his car and went home for his tea.

Stacey Walker (8)
Barnard Castle CE Primary School, Co Durham

A Day In The Life Of A Shop Assistant

One day I was walking to Bayes (that's where I worked). I got the till sorted and opened the shop. People started walking in. When it was time for my friend's coffee break I was all alone in the shop with some customers. I was just typing a man's shopping into the till when I suddenly saw a person that looked a bit like a burglar. I thought I was dreaming. I carried on with everybody's shopping.

When I was finished with all the queue my friend came back with some chocolates.

She said to me, 'Here, you can put some stock into the shop and I'll take over.'

I couldn't really say no so I said, 'OK.'

I went up to the part where stock was kept. I noticed Julie in the shop by herself, she didn't look her best so I started talking to her. We talked for ages till I realised what I was meant to be doing so I said, 'Bye,' to Julie.

I walked around the corner to the stock and got a box of shampoo and brought it downstairs. I came to the shampoo aisle. I saw that man browsing down the aisle. I thought he was hiding something, I didn't dare say anything because he was smirking at me. I finished putting the shampoo in its place and walked quickly down to the till. I rang 999 and a police officer picked up the phone and I told him everything.

The police officer said, 'Oh it will be James Darling, he's escaped prison.'

The policeman came down to Bayes and caught him.

James is in prison longer now and I got £500 for spotting James and my friends never heard what happened that very day.

Fiona Cook (9)
Barnard Castle CE Primary School, Co Durham

Dying Puppies

I crouched down next to my puppies, Zoe wasn't moving on the vet's table. She yelped in pain, I was heartbroken to think she was dying. Waiting, watching the clock - hoping she would live. If I could see her breathing, moving then I would be very happy.

Mary Moore (10)
Barnard Castle CE Primary School, Co Durham

Fairy Godmother

I made a magic potion, it bubbled and mumbled then something happened - *crash!* My potion had exploded, I couldn't move until I had used my magic wand, it twinkled with a little dust and everything was shining like twinkle stars. Then . . . *boom!*

Jade Hadden (10)
Barnard Castle CE Primary School, Co Durham

Gymnast

I flew through the air, I swung over the volt, I felt dizzy, could I take anymore, I could feel myself shaking. I was hot, I twisted round in my flip, it was amazing, everything went blurry, couldn't see anything. It was pitch-black, I fell. Am I alive?

Kelsey-Jade Maughan (10)
Barnard Castle CE Primary School, Co Durham

Orbiting The Earth

I crept into the long grass. I heard whispering - wild, slimy, green men stumbled towards me. I turned - which way should I run? I jerked to the left and skidded to the right, my blood turned cold, my brain filled with fear, my mind went blank. My world had ended.

Louise Lockwood (10)
Barnard Castle CE Primary School, Co Durham

Doctor Danger

A faint light shone through the mucky windows; inside a man stood directly opposite his bubbly pot of dangerous mixtures. A strange sound filled the smoky air, a rumble. Doctor Danger stepped backwards. More smoke filled the air. It spat out a few drips, but then it all exploded.

Laura Hackett (10)
Barnard Castle CE Primary School, Co Durham

The Tragic Accident

Jack and Jill ran up the hill fighting. Suddenly Jack kicked Jill and Jill kicked Jack. The fighting went on until they were both black and blue. Then Jill heaved a gigantic rock up into her arms and dropped it on top of Jack, who rolled down the hill unconscious.

Eve Berry (10)
Barnard Castle CE Primary School, Co Durham

Scary Dad!

Footsteps. Who was it? Dracula! The light went on; I peered under the door. I saw two hairy feet. A snuffly voice called, 'Tom are you in bed?' I opened the door to find Dad standing there wearing his fluffy slippers and holding a tissue over his nose. Oh Dad!

Emily Collings (10)
Barnard Castle CE Primary School, Co Durham

Football

It was coming closer and closer until it hit my foot, then curled round my leg. Suddenly flew back to someone else. I ran away from it as fast as could until . . . *bang!* It hit me in the face. Why is it always me getting hit in the face!

Josh Harper (10)
Barnard Castle CE Primary School, Co Durham

The Murder Story

'Get away from me, I mean it, just leave me alone!' screamed Claire.
  Joe pushed her into a gravestone and dug the knife into Claire. Joe threw her into a ditch and filled it up with soil.
  Ever since, all Joe hears is the beating of the dead girl's heart.

India Ratcliffe (11)
Broughton-in-Furness CE Primary School, Cumbria

Susan The Ghost

Everyone was asleep except Susan. Susan was a ghost. Susan killed her parents for their money and now she was out to get her brother. Susan got to her house. She opened the door and . . . *bang!* Her brother caught her in a ghost catcher and sent her to the Devil!

Helen Satterthwaite (11)
Broughton-in-Furness CE Primary School, Cumbria

Cup Final

Matt played for Hayrigg Rovers and they were 1-0 down in the final.

Matt got the ball on the halfway line and beat two players. The wind blew in his face, he ran. Into the last minute! Matt shot, the ball hit the bar and flopped out. Hayrigg had lost.

Tom Winch (11)
Broughton-in-Furness CE Primary School, Cumbria

Teddy's Lost In A Ditch

In October a biker was cycling on a twisting country lane, when, suddenly, he saw a little girl crying. He asked her what was wrong; she said that she lost her teddy down a ditch. So he got it and cycled her home. Her parents thanked him with great delight.

Joshua Ratcliffe (11)
Broughton-in-Furness CE Primary School, Cumbria

The Present

It was Kelly's birthday and she was waiting for Grandma's present.

On her bed was a book. Kelly hated books. The book was from Grandma! How could Grandma do this?

Kate came in and took it off Kelly. It turned out it was Kate's present and Kelly's hadn't even arrived.

Diane Atkinson (11)
Broughton-in-Furness CE Primary School, Cumbria

The Big Obstacle Course

'Get ready, go.'

Off ran Mouse over a big wide log. Mouse went under the logs easily, but the monkey bars were the hard part, but he managed. He landed into some water and ran for the finishing line. Mouse had come first out of many. He felt really good.

Hayley Robinson (11)
Broughton-in-Furness CE Primary School, Cumbria

Friends In The End

Biller the unicorn and Bubber the frog were fighting. Biller drank water from Bubber's pond, which Bubber didn't allow. Biller and Bubber were fighting with sticks. They were both kind-hearted though and didn't want to hurt anyone. They stopped, mid-fight, they wanted to make friends, so they did.

Emma Garnett (11)
Broughton-in-Furness CE Primary School, Cumbria

Annie's Trip To Grandma's

Annie was going to her granny's one day. Annie knocked on the door. Granny answered it. Annie went inside. They had lots of fun and played games.

Soon it was time for Annie to go home. Little did she know that it was the last. What would Annie do now?

Claudia Bland (11)
Broughton-in-Furness CE Primary School, Cumbria

The Track

Down, I'm going, down the track, it's getting faster, I'm going through the tunnel *argh!* I'm going upside down, spinning, up we go I don't like this, up, up and here we go! Through the loop, wow! Bumps! I don't feel well. I don't like roller coasters, *phew* . . . it's over.

Jacob Frame (11)
Cragside Primary School, Newcastle upon Tyne

A Day In The Life Of Nemo

My dad said that I could go for a swim as long as I did not go far, so I didn't. I was playing dizzy ducklings. As I was spinning I heard a voice saying, 'Nemooo, Nemooo, oh, for God's sake *Nemo!*'

'OK no need to shout Dory.'

She shook her head in confusion. 'Anyway are you coming?'

'Where?' I replied.

'For a wander of course.'

'Oh yes.'

We both went off out in the sea as my dad was sleeping. I went with Dory.

Ten minutes later I squealed, 'Oh no, I've just remembered what my dad said.'

I swam full speed back home, it took about ten minutes and I never even stopped. And *boom!* I crashed but what into? Dory was not there, as she couldn't keep up. I slowly looked up, it was my dad.

'I thought I told you not to go away,' he shouted. 'Grounded, that's what I'll do, I'll ground you for two days. Now I hope you're sorry for what you've just done.'

'I am sorry Dad, please don't ground me.'

He took me home warning me if I did that again I would be grounded for life!

Bobbie-Faye Keelan (11)
Cragside Primary School, Newcastle upon Tyne

The Space Escapade

Kevin clenched his teeth together as he hurtled through the rough asteroid field. The journey had proceeded quite well up until now. Kevin was struggling to even reach the control panel let alone steer his crew to safety.

'Kevin! At the rate our ship is going, landing on Mars is looking quite slim indeed,' expressed Kevin's co-pilot.

'We have to land on a large asteroid or we'll never make it!' Kevin agreed, however it would take up all their fuel, but it was a sacrifice they were willing to make, if they wanted to live.

As each individual set up camp they could feel the unbearable pain of their space boots digging into their ankles. Spirits weren't high.

Suddenly! A terrible sound shrieked in everyone's ears.

'Take cover!' yelled Kevin as he dived under his ship. 'The asteroid belt is breaking!'

'Open the air lock! Get shelter!' shouted the co-pilot.

By now every scrap of food, water and space gear was gone, only the gear the crew were wearing was left, which wasn't good.

'Sir!' demanded the co-pilot.

'Not now Lee!' snapped Kevin.

'But Sir!'

'Not now!'

'If you want to live please listen! This particular asteroid is made of a similar substance to our ship's fuel. If the crew can co-operate this is possible.'

So in went most of the asteroid, while Kevin and Lee started the engines.

As the crew staggered in, the ship rocketed off, it was a close shave, however, would they be as lucky next time?

Julian Wyton (11)
Cragside Primary School, Newcastle upon Tyne

Typhoon

'The air is dusty here, the desert must be clear,' exclaimed Udah. 'We must be getting close now.'

Udah was one of those middle-aged men who had a taste for adventure. He was tall and had quite an unusual look to his face. His mother had always said he was one of a kind.

This particular day he was on his way to Volosae in search of a most precious jewel, alongside him was his assistant Jamal Sindle.

They were travelling through the Typhoon Desert, which was famous for its lack of water and world famous sandstorms.

'I think I see it,' shouted Jamal.

'See what?' asked Udah, with an astonished tone to his voice.

'The cave where the landstone is,' replied the young assistant, 'let's run.'

The cave was damp and dark; it had a distinctive smell to it.

'Get the lamps out,' ordered Udah. 'It is time to search for our goal.'

The pair searched the cave from top to bottom but they saw neither head nor tail of the landstone's glint.

The lamps started to fail when Jamal called out, 'I can see it, the landstone's shine!'

'Yes!' yelled Udah.

Then there came a rumble from deep inside the cave. Unexpectedly some rocks fell from the cave's roof.

'Rock fall!' shouted the young explorer. *'Get out of here.'*

They sprinted for the exit but a huge boulder fell and blocked the way.

There was no way out. They were trapped.

Neil Davies (11)
Cragside Primary School, Newcastle upon Tyne

A Day In The Life Of Tracy Beaker

'Dear Mum,

I want you to know, if you don't know, it is my birthday on the 8th September. If I had one wish, I'd wish you would come and take me away to Hollywood, I've been telling Justine, Louise and the rest, but they don't believe me, so make my wish come true.

Love Tracy.'

Tracy was writing to her mum, everyone was planning a surprise 12th birthday for her downstairs in the garden, it wasn't till Saturday but they wanted to be ready.

Breakfast/Tracy's birthday

'Has the post come yet?'

'Yes Tracy it is waiting on the table for you,' said Shelly.

'Open it then,' Louise said.

Tracy opened it very slowly and it said . . .

'Dear Tracy,

Sorry I can't come and take you out on your birthday I need to go to a very important place but I promise another time.

Love Mum.'

'It's from my mum.'

'It is not!' Justine said.

'Fine, then believe what you want!' shouted Tracy.

Later

'Come on we have a surprise for you downstairs,' said Shelly.

Bedtime

'I'm going to write to my mum before I go to bed.'

'OK then,' said Shelly.

'Dear Mum,

Thank you for the birthday card and letter, Shelly, Duke and rest did a surprise party for me, and Justine was finally nice to me, the party was the best, wish you were there, that would have been even better. Love Tracy.

PS Missing you very much and come back for me soon.'

Jenna Ferguson (11)
Cragside Primary School, Newcastle upon Tyne

A Day In The Life Of A Hacker

Everything started when Samuel was introduced to networking, he was only eleven, but loved computers.

Samuel was tall, with blond hair and blue eyes.

One day he used a program called 'Telnet' to connect to his dad's laptop and control it, but, eventually Samuel wanted to go further . . .

. . . Samuel decided he would steal some valuable data from the FBI database. he typed 'WHOIS:FBI' and hit return, he soon received results. 'WHOIS LOOK UP

FBI Internal Services System

IP:176.45.38.177'.

Sam ran a portscan,

'PSCAN:127.45.38.177

Open ports on:176.45.38.177

22 MISC

80 TCPIP

21 TELNET.

He connected to port 80 (TCPIP) by inputting: 'CONNECT;176.45.38.177:80' and he was in! Sam wanted to download data on the Apollo 11 landing, but couldn't be bothered to search for it so he guessed: 'DOWNLOAD:C\DATA\APOLLO'

'INVALID DIRECTORY' flashed on the screen, then another message: *'You have been traced and will be prosecuted in about one minute.'*

Samuel's heart started to thump, he didn't know what to do, then there was a knock at the door . . .

Samuel Kennedy (11)
Cragside Primary School, Newcastle upon Tyne

Game Over

I kept running. The man with the knife kept chasing me. I ran through the dark passageway, I'd never been here before. It was pitch-black; I turned on my torch. There wasn't just one man but five. They drew their knives. Then the dreaded words came . . . 'Game over!'

Connor Brown (11)
Cragside Primary School, Newcastle upon Tyne

The Scam

Sam Phillips is the boy that everyone knew after the devious scam he brought about on March 20th. It all started when Sam's dad was promoted to head of the SATs co-operation, he had every bit of information about all the questions and answers in old tests and new tests.

March 17th

It was a dark and stormy night, Sam's mum was telling Sam to revise for the SATs but, he wasn't listening, he was gripped to his new computer game, 'Ghostblasters' it had just come out so everyone wanted it.

March 18th

Sam's dad was away at a conference in London and left his laptop, Sam was on his computer game, he was on the seventh level. Sam's mum came in and told him to revise, he wasn't listening so she turned the computer off. Sam was in a mood from school after his teacher kept him in from lunch to learn his 14 times table.

March 19th

It was 8pm, Sam's dad still wasn't back. Sam was playing on his dad's laptop, when he received an email, Sam opened it, it was the answers for the SATs; he decided to print it out and use it for the test next day.

March 20th

It was the morning, the teacher had set the tables out, Sam had the answers, or so he thought . . .

June 29th

They all had their own envelopes with their results. Sam opened his, it had straight level 3s. He had printed out last year's test sheet!

Ben Goldie (11)
Cragside Primary School, Newcastle upon Tyne

A Day In The Life As Justine Littlewood

I hate that Tracy Beaker, everyone thinks she's the best just because she's got a new, modern, up-to-date mobile phone, and Jenny said that I spent all of my money on sweets and CDs. But I didn't, it was Louise who persuaded me to get that new CD and try out the sweets that had just been advertised. There was £120 in my money tin when I started, now there's only £6.75 left. It's all Louise's fault. I bet you £1,000,000 that she's already took some money out, *to borrow,* she normally says and then she says 'I'll give you it back', she never does. Anyway by the time I save up I'm going to get the newest and a much better mobile than Tracy Beaker.

Meanwhile back at the Dumping Ground Tracy wasn't letting anyone touch her *new* mobile she said she was the only one allowed to play on the games, text, and phone friends on it. (Justine and Louise entered through the door.)

And as soon as I walked in the Dumping Ground with Lou, can you guess what I saw? Tracy Beaker showing off her new mobile phone with *my* friends, all seven of them, sitting and playing with the person they all apparently didn't like. Sitting there with my chocolates I got from *my* dad. *'What have you done!'* I screamed I snatched the chocolates off them and ran upstairs, and as always Louise was following. *I hate that Tracy Beaker!*

Gabrielle Armstrong (10)
Cragside Primary School, Newcastle upon Tyne

Cave Times

I woke up.

'Ug ug,' my mother shouted. She wanted a bucket of water.

I took the bucket to the lake and filled it. I was on my way home when I began to sink in quicksand. A mammoth came and helped me. I took him home. We roasted him.

Conor Reichal (11)
Cragside Primary School, Newcastle upon Tyne

Beyond

I manoeuvred in. Ready and eager to launch into unfamiliar territory and explore new dimensions. Not knowing the fear that I might not return from this dangerous, daring mission. Suddenly, flames stampeded out from the massive seven foot exhausts. My adrenaline kicked in and I was off into space.

Jonathan Snell (11)
Cragside Primary School, Newcastle upon Tyne

People Run

Sam ran faster and faster, down to his destination outdoors, followed by Kelly. They heard a funny noise upstairs. They looked up, it was Sammy, their old cat creeping down the stairs. They went down the rest of the stairs from room 190, getting further towards their destination.

Madeleine O'Hara (10)
Cragside Primary School, Newcastle upon Tyne

The Legend Of Orlandrino And Trespisnastious

Long, long ago there was a brave fighter called Orlandrino. She was a great warrior and loved her people. One day she was sent away to join forces with another country for a great battle, but she didn't know where she was going, so she and her crew ended up deserted on a strange island.

It was gloomy, dark and you could smell brimstone. Suddenly they heard a noise, it sounded like one of Orlandrino's men crying, 'Help, help Trespisnastious!'

Orlandrino ran round the corner and found one of her men hypnotised by a huge camouflaged monster. Suddenly it disappeared, all that was left in that place was a lamb.

Later Orlandrino reached an old ruin which had a river of fire on one side and a river of water on the other. Then all of a sudden appeared Trespisnastious blowing fire out of his mouth. The flames charged at Orlandrino like a dragon, she grabbed an old snake's tail skin and filled it with water then threw it at the fire. The fire suddenly disappeared and Orlandrino filled another tail skin with water and threw it at the ugly, smelly monster.

Orlandrino's men were silent because, the monster had spellbound them. Orlandrino told Trespisnastious to give their speech back. Then with that she threw the water at him and he collapsed to the ground in a seething puddle of foam. They left the island and thought they saw home but was it?

Madeleine Macaulay (11)
Cragside Primary School, Newcastle upon Tyne

A Day In The Life Of Tracy Beaker

I hate Justine Littlewood because she wouldn't let me play on her new mobile phone, she said I had to pay her £1 for five minutes. Just because her dad is going to Spain for a month he bought a phone so she could keep in touch with him.

Every child at Stowy House, my care home, was invited to Katie's party but we have to have permission from a parent or guardian. I was going to ask Cam, my old foster mum, but she's in France, and Jenny said I can't ring her!

Katie was my friend from school and she said I didn't need permission, but Jenny my care worker said I did. The party is tomorrow at four o'clock, after school.

That night I couldn't get to sleep because I love discos, and I couldn't let everyone else go and not me! Eventually I fell asleep, well for five minutes. Then Louise woke me up and said I could get permission from her auntie, but her auntie is not my auntie!

Next morning I was so tired because I'd hardly had any sleep. I asked Jenny, Duke and even Elaine the Pain. Then when I was eating some toast I had a brainwave. I could ask Ben's mum because even Ben's going, I couldn't wait to ask her.

I was allowed to go and even Jenny was persuaded! So now I'm at the party having a great time!

Lauren Matthewson (11)
Cragside Primary School, Newcastle upon Tyne

Sweat

I was standing in the middle of the field, waiting for my friends when suddenly a cold hand draped across my neck, I felt a cool breeze blow my hair from behind. Was it the wolf that everyone talked about? I turned and no one was there.

Louise Hollingsworth (11)
Cragside Primary School, Newcastle upon Tyne

The Night That Changed My Life Forever

The black in front of me was like a shield from this world to that. I stood stunned, like a frozen block of ice. The lights were beating down on me, melting me. Sweat was running down my face. I waited patiently for the words, was it me, or was it him? Then suddenly I thought, *it is my turn to speak.* I spoke slowly, the words came out all wrong. 'No, you're a . . . thief! Thief!' The big red cloth came down, I was saved. I ran to my dressing room and wiped the sweat from my face.

That night at the theatre everything had gone wrong. The stage door was wide open, hundreds of people were there, cameras were flashing in my face, was it a dream? Suddenly somebody called my name, 'Chris! Chris!' I turned and there was a news team, they were asking me all sorts of questions. Like for instance, 'How did you feel when the crowd went wild after your performance?' I thought for a moment, I thought that I was terrible. I wasn't though.

I was going to make the front page. Film directors were at the door asking me to be in *blockbuster* films!

That night was the best night I had ever had! But now I *am* in *blockbuster* films. That experience will never be removed from my mind.

However, that reminds me of the night I went to the Oscars, but that's another story.

Chris Mole (11)
Cragside Primary School, Newcastle upon Tyne

Fear

His eyes glinted with fear, the worst thing in the world was just outside his front door.

It all started one day when the doorbell rang at six o'clock in the morning. Ben was the only person awake in the house, combing his black hair. Therefore, he ran downstairs to see who it was. A man shouted through the brass letter box, 'Urgent letter here!' Phew, it was the postman.

The letter dropped through the letter box. Ben picked up the letter and opened it. His worst fear was coming. Tomorrow. Ben stood there petrified. The last time she came he ended up with a really scary thing.

'Now she's here I'm gonna die.' It was Grandma.

James Hedley (11)
Cragside Primary School, Newcastle upon Tyne

Race For Time

Alex started, palms sweating, he felt a rush of adrenaline, he was going to finish it, he could tell. Then came the dreaded words, 'One minute.' His hope sank, he was all for failing, but then inspiration struck, he jotted it down. He sighed, he had finally finished the test!

Madoc Flynn (11)
Cragside Primary School, Newcastle upon Tyne

A Day In The Life Of Harry Potter

Aunt Petunia told me to get up and make the breakfast for Dudley's 15th birthday. I got up, he kicked me and pushed past me, I went to the kitchen.

'I want everything perfect or you'll have no meals for a week,' said Uncle Vernon.

'Yes Uncle Vernon,' I replied. When he turned around I shot him a dirty glare.

I took the breakfast over to Dudley.

'Yuck! This is horrible tell him to make better stuff now!'

I got up and made him some eggs, bacon and toast. I took it over.

'I said nicer stuff, this is even worse!'

'Dudley eat it now and stop being awkward, when your mum makes it you enjoy it so eat it.'

He ate it all, stuffing his face.

After I ate breakfast I did the dishes then someone rang the doorbell. I got up and answered the door, it was one of Dudley's friends.

'Come in,' shouted Dudley.

I went to my room and then I was called by Aunt Petunia. I ran, there was a lovely smell, it was kipper, it was for our tea.

We started to eat about five minutes later, when Dudley suddenly started to choke. Uncle Vernon jumped up, he pulled Dudley up, he heaved him up and pushed his stomach and Aunt Petunia grabbed a slice of bread and shoved it in his mouth. He stopped choking and Uncle Vernon took Dudley's friend home after that and at about nine o'clock we went to bed.

Joshua Oliver (11)
Cragside Primary School, Newcastle upon Tyne

The Black Creature

I thought it was gone. I raced onwards seeing the misty sky clearer and clearer. I knew I was nearly home. I didn't think it had stopped following me, but it did. I was relieved that I was now at my own front door. Safe and sound but was I? The house was empty, there was no sound at all, I went upstairs to see if anyone was there but the place was deserted. This had happened before.

Two weeks ago they went out without telling me. But they always leave a note on the fridge though, so I will be fine sat on the sofa watching TV.

They had been gone three hours now. I didn't know they would be this long but I supposed they're having a good time so I waited and waited but there was no sign of them at all. Then suddenly I heard a knock at the door. I thought that it would be them but it wasn't. I opened the door, standing there was that thing that followed me home, the black, slimy, slithering thing that crept all over me.

I slammed the door on it screaming. I ran upstairs and locked the bathroom door panting like mad . . .

Ashley Hildyard (11)
Cragside Primary School, Newcastle upon Tyne

The Bunny With Gas

It was the night before Easter, a strange smell crept up the stairs. As I made my way down the stairs the smell got stronger and stronger, as I opened the door I heard a giggle. Then I noticed a lop ear hanging over the sofa, I made my way further into the room and it was a really incredible sight. It was the Easter bunny and he had pumped. Yet again he pumped the air turned green. I ran out of the room and burst out laughing without a care in the world let alone in my house.

Then my baby sister started to cry, I grabbed the bunny and stuck him in the vase and hid him in the shadows. Then my mum burst through the door with a very nasty face on. 'Get to bed or the bunny won't come.'

Then the bunny pumped and the vase smashed.

'Did this have anything to do with you?'

Uh-oh!

Nathan Harwood (11)
Cragside Primary School, Newcastle upon Tyne

The Place

It was freezing, shivers went like lightning down his spine. He was scared, no terrified. The howling and crying drummed in and out of his head, it was too much. He never went there again.

Andrew Watson (11)
Cragside Primary School, Newcastle upon Tyne

Sirens

The sirens went off, I jumped up, my little brother looked around in shock. My mum rushed into my room. She grabbed my arm and my brother's arm and ran outside. She was panicking but I don't think she wanted to show it, she shoved us in the bomb shelter and locked the doors.

My little brother was crying, I was hiding under my pillow, the bombs were coming down so heavy the shelter was rattling. My mother said I shouldn't be scared now because I'm 10 but I still have dreams that my mother will go away from me and my brother. My father is away at war and my mother worries that she cannot cope and that was why I was scared all the time.

Samantha McNally (11)
Cragside Primary School, Newcastle upon Tyne

The Death Of Violet

It was my first day of being a servant at 10 years old, my name is Violet and I look after the Astons at 20 Cannon Road.

I woke up at 5am, my first job was to get the Astons' breakfast. I hardly had any sleep because of the damp sheets and creaky floorboards. The draught from the doors gave me shivers up my spine; I never felt right all day. The Astons sent me for another job to tidy the kitchen however, the kitchen was a disgrace, and I washed the floor. I did not want to do it, so Mr Aston hit me.

I did not have anything to eat, they watched telly all day while I was doing work. I wanted to escape, I decided I would. I packed all of my belongings, I was going to escape out of the window.

The window was broad, I stood on the ledge and worked my way down until I heard the crackle of pebbles, I ran so that nobody could see me. There were many roads, I did not look left or right, I carried on running until I reached the motorway.

Wind was whistling through my hair. I waited until it was clear. I could not think, I felt dizzy with the noise. Suddenly I was hit; I heard sirens coming closer to me that was when I knew I was gone.

Rachel Darby (10)
Cragside Primary School, Newcastle upon Tyne

The Hooded Hallowe'en

I jumped to my feet, as a hooded figure slid into my room, leaving a trail of scarlet blood as it went. From out of the blue, it grabbed a scythe. It dropped its hood.

'Happy Hallowe'en!' said my brother with a smug grin.

Zak Hubbard (11)
Cragside Primary School, Newcastle upon Tyne

The Devastation

It was 5.30 when I woke up this morning. I had to travel to Scotland to see my father, from my house in Wales. My mum had to get my younger brothers and sisters ready. I have four brothers and three sisters, I'm the oldest, I'm 11. I do all the hard work in my house, because my mum is having another baby. She's got another two weeks to go before I have a new brother or sister. All the family is looking forward to the baby that's why my father is coming home because he wants to be here when the baby is born. That means I'll have to look after the children while my mum and dad are away.

Three weeks later my mum came back crying. My youngest sisters Claire said, 'Where's the baby?'

My mum replied, 'There's no baby . . . it died!'

My youngest sister didn't understand what that meant. Then my mum went to lie down, depressed. She said to me quietly, 'The baby was a girl, we were going to call her Emily Elizabeth Jones.'

Sarah-Jay Davidson (11)
Cragside Primary School, Newcastle upon Tyne

The Horror

The horror. The horror. I couldn't stand it. Just the sight of it scared me. I just wanted to get away. It was the most horrible thing I'd ever seen. My grandma's egg and chips. Then the doorbell rang. I answered it. It was my dad. I was saved.

Barney Wallace (11)
Cragside Primary School, Newcastle upon Tyne

The Danger Ride!

I was there! Right in front of my eyes, I was so excited, and full of joy. There were hundreds of them. Roller coasters, waltzers, even Big Ben. I was at The Hoppings. I wasn't interested in the baby rides, even though my mum as begging me to.

'Amy why don't you go on this one!' yelled Dad.

I turned around to find my dad pointing at the Distracter. A ride that might look fine, however it could break your neck.

I turned and walked away, but I was too late, my dad had grabbed my arm. He had already bought the tickets for me. Just me! I stumbled as I walked up the stairs to a seat. The ride started. I was already upside down, going upwards. Without warning, I zoomed down clutching onto my seat, screaming and shouting!

We were falling in thin air, I could not gasp for help, I was going so fast my heart was in my stomach, in floods of tears we landed. Struggling to get out I shouted, cried but I could not think because of all the people screaming. I sat there in pain waiting for someone to help. At last I heard the siren coming towards us. 'Help!' I cried. I fainted in distress.

A few moments later, I woke up on the ground. I was out at last from the ride that I dreaded to suffer on.

Ruby Catherall (11)
Cragside Primary School, Newcastle upon Tyne

The Unknown Mask

It had all started on a dark, gloomy night. The shrieking of an owl bellowed into Vanessa's ears. Vanessa, the most intelligent girl in school, was walking home late because she was on detention.

Minute by minute, dawn was dusk. She was just round the corner from her house when something caught her attention. A figure fading away into the distance!

Leaving her house behind, she walked on. Vanessa thought it might be her friends trying to scare her as it was Hallowe'en. When she got there, no one was there. As she was just about to walk out she saw something shining at the tip of her eyes. It had thin white string-like hair and red spots. She turned it around, it was a mask! Now she would wear it and scare her friends.

As she put it on, it felt strange. The mask was gluing onto her face. Vanessa was pulling it off but it wouldn't come off. She was shouting for help, her voice was becoming croaky and old.

After months of searching for Vanessa, she was never heard of again.

Two years later, 'Mummy look! A scary mask, argh!'

Farijan Begum Sufi (11)
Cragside Primary School, Newcastle upon Tyne

The Shadow

I ran down the road, my stomach ached, the shadow glided towards me. I ran down a street. *Dead end!*

It was after me, I had nowhere to go, the hooded black cloak rippled in the wind. The figure took off its hood. 'Bath time!' my mom laughed evilly.

Joe Withers (11)
Cragside Primary School, Newcastle upon Tyne

The Forbidden Castle

It was scary, the moss, the uncut grass, with a big rusty gate which squeaked when you opened it.

I walked in and shouted, 'Is anyone home?' No answer. I looked round. The bedrooms had king-sized beds. I was on my way out, a shadow stood in the doorway!

Alex Fawcett (11)
Cragside Primary School, Newcastle upon Tyne

Spirits On The Beach

Lola and her friends walked across the misty beach.

What had been the summer beach bash had turned into a grey misty night. Lola turned her head to look for light when she saw a girl. She was standing by the sea, crying out words, 'Mist clear please, so that I can see the spirits.' Lola turned to her friends but they were gone. She looked behind her and then she saw them. The spirits! Each of them were crying the same words as the girl. Lola was puzzled because the spirits were next to each other but they couldn't see.

Lola walked up to the spirit girl. She reached out her hand to touch her. Lola's hand went right through her. Her hand turned a pale blue, she screamed but her voice was drained.

Suddenly bright lights shone and blinded Lola. The spirits ran and disappeared into the mist as a white van moved slowly towards Lola. The van stopped. Lola looked in the window but there was no one there. She turned and started to journey to find her friends thinking about the spirits all the way.

Sarah Robinson (11)
Cragside Primary School, Newcastle upon Tyne

The Flood

Water gushed into my house, seeping through my trainers, swirling round and round my feet. I tried to cover up cracks where it might come in but that made matters worse and more water burst in. I was now knee-deep in it. Why was I so scared of water?

Sarah Henderson (11)
Cragside Primary School, Newcastle upon Tyne

Spirits Of The Sea

The cold air whipped the roaring waves against the rocks. With her scarf blowing fiercely in the gales, Sian stood at the edge of the cliff. In her hand she clutched what looked like a clock. 'They will never find you!' she whimpered. Then she threw it into the dark blue water below.

'Sian! Please pay attention!' bellowed Miss Redall.

Her eyes were fixed on the sea. She picked up her bag and walked to the door. 'I'm feeling ill.'

Leaving the school behind her she decided to visit the lighthouse. The winter sky was now a dark purple and the street lamps were lit. Suddenly, lights loomed out of the darkness. A ship was coming aport. It was wood and old, Sian waved her hands high in the air and within minutes the ship had sailed towards her. A small glowing figure strolled up to her, its hands were grasping gold. The watch! Sian lunged at the immortal, only to fall into the ocean.

The cold sea was wrapping around Sian, drowning her. The child was gone. She was falling deeper and deeper and her heartbeat slowed down.

Sian awoke gasping for air, once again she was back on land with her watch beside her.

Amy Louise Biwer (11)
Cragside Primary School, Newcastle upon Tyne

The Ride Of Doom

My body shook with fear as I saw it go round in circles. As I watched it, I stumbled up the stairs and once I got to the top, I stopped. I walked and got into it, it started to move. I was scared to the bone of roller coasters.

Simon Anderson (11)
Cragside Primary School, Newcastle upon Tyne

Scarlet's Warning Adventure

It was dark and a strange night. The winding roads whipped all the cold and frosty snow away. Scarlet somehow felt that it wasn't a normal night in London. Her hair flashed like golden stars. It was her twelfth birthday, June 13th 1972. She wished she had never had it now.

It was quiet . . . silent like paint drying. Plodding in the streets of London with all her might, she felt cold icicles up her spine, her feet like damp cotton wool.

She stopped gradually and saw a flickering bright light straight in front of her. At that moment, Scarlet walked slowly towards it. A few seconds later she was swung up in the dark sky and landed near a strange school. She cautiously walked closer and closer towards it. Suddenly an extremely pale-faced figure from nowhere appeared and was grinning. Then all of a sudden, her voice squeaked, she seemed familiar to Scarlet, had she seen her from somewhere?

'Hullo my dear, don't be afraid. I must warn you, you mustn't go on your trip, the plane is doomed to crash! Go back and warn your family!'

She finally got home, Scarlet was helping to pack in the attic with her mother and father. The old dusty photo album flew open and there in front of her was the pale, white face . . . her great grandmother! What was she to do now?

Lisa Waggett (11)
Cragside Primary School, Newcastle upon Tyne

Harry Potty

One day Chris was talking to his mum about Harry Potty, the giant ant.
 Chris's mum was saying that Harry Potty was too big for the shoe. Then the doorbell rang, Harry Potty was saved.

Christopher Richardson (11)
Cragside Primary School, Newcastle upon Tyne

The Haunted House

Black clouds gathered around while something terrifying comes my way.

I am in my house all by myself as I've just come home from Italy and lying there is my best friend David. He doesn't look alive, as blood is racing out of his head. I couldn't help him, it is too risky. He would not stop shaking. Even worse, my phone is broken and I'm scared to go out of my house that's risky too because that person or animal might attack me.

I thought about shouting for help but then again I might get killed if they hear me. I've got two worries on my mind now. One from David's parents and one from my parents wondering how David died.

Ten days after his death it's David's funeral and me and my parents went. David's mother Lisa, stared at me as if I'd committed a crime. She came over to me - I had to keep my head up and face what was coming to me. It wasn't looking good so far because she gave me a look of hatred which got me really scared, but I don't understand I didn't kill him. It's my house, it must be haunted or something. Two days later my mum was attacked in my house again. She's in intensive care fighting for her life.

First it's David and now it's my mum, I can't put up with it. I have only got my dad left.

Andy Lee Robertson (11)
Cragside Primary School, Newcastle upon Tyne

Sam's Red Phone

Sam was taking a walk round the park when her phone rang. She looked up at the sky, it was very dark, she put one hand into her handbag and she suddenly realised that there was a phone thief on the loose.

She felt in her bag again, but it wasn't there anymore. Sam's leg shook, her hair on the back of her neck stuck up. She followed the ringing, it led her to the bushes near the pond. Her heart raced when she saw a strange-looking figure. She walked towards it, feeling more and more scared, but then as she turned the corner she saw an old man with about sixty phones in the dark corner. Then a ragged figure came from out of the distance and into the corner.

'Wait! May I have my phone back please?' Then her phone was thrown at her and from that day on, no one bothered her again for her phone.

Faye Armstrong (11)
Cragside Primary School, Newcastle upon Tyne

The Race

Poppy was in the lead and Lucy was way behind. They were in a race and puffing and panting badly. Poppy was nearly at her destination. She arrived breathless and won the prize which was a bike and a trophy. Lucy and Madeleine were angry and frustrated and very jealous.

Kerry-Anne Eileen Browne (10)
Cragside Primary School, Newcastle upon Tyne

The Two Clowns And The Time Machine

There once were two men called Bill and Ben, they were twins, stupid twins. Anyway that was all proved on their trip to see what it would be like in the past.

It's not a book, it's a gizmo shop owned by Professor Dave, he's a crazy scientist but he makes really cool gadgets, anyway let's get on with the story . . .

They got up early as usual to see if Professor Dave had made any new gadgets. Bill and Ben were eating breakfast when something came through the letter box. 'Get the paper stupid,' said Ben.

'Who are you calling stupid, stupid?' replied Bill.

They both got up and went to Dave's he was testing something. 'What are you making Dave?' asked Ben.

'A time machine,' said Dave

'Where's the old one?' asked Bill.

'It's with all the other devices that didn't work,' said Dave.

'And where is that?'

'In the bin,' said Dave.

'Well is the new one nearly done?' asked Ben.

'Yes it is as a matter of fact. I'm going out the back, so don't touch a thing or else something bad might happen.' Dave walked out the back of the gizmo shop.

'What did he say?' asked Ben.

'I don't know, anyway let's try it out,' said Bill.

'I don't know!' said Ben.

'What, you chicken?' asked Bill.

'No, it's that you're so stupid, you don't know what it could do,' replied Ben.

'It's a time machine, you idiot,' said Bill.

'Now that's no way to talk about yourself,' laughed Ben.

Dave came in and Ben swung his fist, missed Bill and hit Dave and then Dave fell into the time machine.

'Argh!'

Matthew Phillips (11)
Cragside Primary School, Newcastle upon Tyne

The Horrible Day

The day was misty and cloudy and the clouds started to rain. It was getting heavier and heavier. I got soaked. I had to go in to dry myself, then it stopped and when I went back outside again, it had started raining. Then I went back and sat inside the house.

Samantha Baker (11)
Cragside Primary School, Newcastle upon Tyne

The Horror Of The Unicorn Ride

I was in Orlando, Florida, where I was near some awesome rides. I was in the Islands of Adventure and I think that it's the best park. I was getting nervous and I was only in line for the Unicorn. I was in horror, horror, it was horrible.

I was cranking up in the cart. The drop, it was too high, it was two feet. Sweat rolled down my face, I trembled and trembled. By the time I'd got over the pain, the ride was over. I felt ridiculous when I got off. All it was was a tiny drop and swerve round and it then finished. I laughed, after all the pain I'd gone through for that ride!

I was walking around laughing until suddenly I approached the biggest roller coaster in the whole park. It would seem that I would have no chance to go on it. But I just started to think about it. I thought I couldn't do it, not to mention the fact that I was scared on the Unicorn ride.

Inside queuing looked scarier than the roller coaster itself, it wasn't pleasant. Then a minute later one of the staff said that I was too small for it. He said I could go to the front of any queue for any ride I wanted, and of course it was the . . . yes, you've guessed it. *The Unicorn!*

Jake Fothergill (11)
Cragside Primary School, Newcastle upon Tyne

The Fabulous Four

In the near future there lived four creatures. They are Donkey, Dominic, Puss In Boots and Jonny English. Their evil nemesis was Griffster who led the alien Chesney Bats who lived in the core of the sun. The four creatures lived in an enchanted forest protected and filled with mythical beasts.

All of the four creatures lived very peacefully in their forest but one dark, gloomy night at the stroke of midnight the alien Chesney Bats abducted Donkey and Puss.

The next morning Jonny woke up to find them missing, so he checked everywhere in the forest (even down the toilet).

Then Dominic woke up and Jonny said, 'Donkey and Puss are missing!'

Dominic replied, 'They were probably abducted by the alien Chesney Bats and Lapacatatoto (the second in command) is conducting experiments on them.'

'What!' Jonny screamed.

'I will save them,' Dominic said.

Ten minutes later Jonny received a message from Dominic saying, 'Help I'm captured!'

Jonny then said, 'So now what's he gone and done, getting himself captured. Looks like it's up to me!'

So Jonny got the space shuttle to the sun and took the entrance to the sun's core. He got to the entrance of the dungeon and bribed the guard with a lollipop, then went to defeat the alien Chesney Bats. Lapacatatoto committed suicide and the Chesney Bats disintegrated, and Griffster was shot by Dominic. Then the sun melted to sludge and they became 'The Fabulous Four'.

Dominic Donkin (10)
Greenland Junior School, Co Durham

World War II Experience

I'm Rebekah and I'll tell you my story.

It all started when we were all on a nice trip to a history museum, it started off with some boring things we couldn't be bothered to look at. But a World War II display suddenly caught our eye and we decided to look a little longer. Suddenly, Raigan, Janine and me were pulled in and landed on the floor - we were in World War II.

'How are we here?' shouted Raigan.

Suddenly a soldier pulled all of us and took us away. We kicked and screamed but he wouldn't let us go. We then realised we were being put in a concentration camp.

'We'll have to run away,' said Janine, worrying.

'We'll have to,' I said.

Raigan looked around, there was a sewage pipe. 'We could climb through the sewage pipe,' Raigan said.

So we all climbed through the gunge and the grime which was unbelievable. We finally slid out, we were panting and were covered in gunge. We quickly climbed over the gate, we were out! Not just out of the concentration camp but out of World War II! We all looked forward and saw our class ahead of us.

'What took you so long?' someone asked.

We all said, 'You wouldn't believe us if we told you!'

Emily Thynne (10)
Greenland Junior School, Co Durham

The Russian Dummy

It all started when we got on the bus to go to the museum. When we got there I wandered off to this ancient World War I exhibition. I started to look at this army dummy when suddenly the dummy grabbed me and pulled me in.

Then he disappeared and I was in Russia, then this army person came out of nowhere and said in Russian, 'Who are you?'

I didn't know what to say, so I just kept quiet, then I said something by accident and he took me to this strange place. It was in the middle of nowhere and I was dying of thirst. Then the man said to me in English, 'You will die!'

I panicked and tried to untie the ropes behind my back. Sweat dripped from my hands but I couldn't untie the ropes and I knew I was going to die soon. I was lined up, ready to be shot then he came with a machine gun and slowly pulled the trigger. I felt the shot go through me.

Then I was amazed to find that I was alive and back in the museum.

Rebekah West (10)
Greenland Junior School, Co Durham

Untitled

One fine summer's day there were four men called Shay Given, Alan Shearer, Bobby Robson and Steve Harper. They all had to go to St James' Park for a special presentation for being the best players and best manager of the season

Later that day, before the presentation, it started to rain and thunder, so they went to Old Trafford but it started lightning so they went to the Stadium of Light. It was very big inside but it started to rain, so they went back St James' Park where it was sunny. They had their presentation as the sun shone down right on the top of the trophy.

This goes to show that the sun always shines on St James'!

Jamie Caisley (10)
Greenland Junior School, Co Durham

Love At First Sight

One fine day when the sun was shining and the birds were tweeting, there was a man called Dominic and a woman called Emily. They bumped into each other on the street, then he offered her a meal at a very rich and posh restaurant. When they were having their meal, Emily asked Dominic if he would go out with her, he replied, 'Yes!'

After the meal they decided to stop at Dominic's house and when they got there Dominic cracked open a bottle of champagne and then as they were drinking it, it was like a love potion. They both looked deeply into each other's eyes and they got closer together and started to kiss each other. Then at midnight, Emily told Dominic she had to go home.

The next day she came over to see him and they kept doing the same thing over and over again for six months until Dominic asked Emily, 'Will you marry me?'

Emily replied, 'Yes I will!'

After the wedding Emily was going to have a baby - it was twins! When they were born she called the boy Simon and the girl Laura. The children grew, but when they got older they didn't move to a new house. Simon had a girlfriend and Laura had a boyfriend but they were so afraid that if they moved away to a new house, something would happen to their mother and father.

Alex Jobson (10)
Greenland Junior School, Co Durham

Discovery Museum

As I went into the Discovery Museum with my friends I felt quite dizzy. But after dinner I felt alright and we asked our teacher if we could go to the gift shop. She said yes, so off we went when that dizzy feeling suddenly came back over me.

Then I obviously fainted because I had this weird feeling that I had disappeared into space and had reached the cold blue sky. I can remember that it was so cold I could barely feel my toes. I thought I'd frozen still and couldn't move because I'd got stuck. It seemed like a million years that I was frozen in that dark empty space. Then suddenly I was back in the museum.

Everything looked so weird. People were walking around in spacesuits with sunglasses on and nobody could talk English. I had been transported to the future and I was still only ten.

No one believed me when I told them what 2004 was like.

Roshni Miah (10)
Greenland Junior School, Co Durham

The Fairy Ball

The fairy got ready for a party in a new spider-silk dress. As she fell on her moss blanket, her head fell on her petal pillow. 'How shall we get there?' she asked.

'By butterfly carriage,' her boyfriend said. 'My love, let's go.' He was in a rose petal suit.

They danced at the Beetle Ball. They danced and danced and at the stroke of midnight the door opened and her boyfriend's dad sent him onto the stage. Her boyfriend asked her, 'Will you marry me?'

'Yes I will!'

They lived happily ever after in the trunk of a tree.

Amy Halliday (10)
Greenland Junior School, Co Durham

A Dog's Life

I am walking quickly to my water bowl and eating my food. Mmm steak flavour. Slowly I walk and sit at the door and wait for someone to let me out.

Uh-oh, here comes something, I'll have to do it in here! Argh, here it comes, that's better.

Now it's time to get some petting up.

Oh no Mummy's going upstairs I hope she doesn't see the poop!

'Naughty boy Wally. The dog needs taking out now!'

Oh no, lazy Larry, he'll only go to the garden gate and fall asleep. I sort of feel worried in case sweet Suzy won't like me anymore.

Jade Sutton (10)
Greenland Junior School, Co Durham

What Cats Get Up To When They're Alone

It was a cold, dark night. Cip, a cat, was messing up the house. The fridge was open and everything was on the floor. The bin was knocked over and the house was a mess.

Suddenly a cat came from nowhere.

'Who are you?' asked Cip shaking his paws.

'I'm Salem, I'm the new cat that lives here,' said the cat.

'Can we clean up?'

'Yes!' said Cip.

Because the house was such a mess in the morning, it was still so messy.

Ring! Ring!

'It's the people, hurry up!'

They pushed all the stuff back in the bin and back in the fridge and went to bed. Just in time - phew!

Tamara Brown (10)
Greenland Junior School, Co Durham

The Simpsons

My life begins when I'm at home watching The Simpsons.

One day I suddenly fell into a big adventure. I was in the TV on the Simpsons' program! I came out dressed up as Krusty the Clown. No one else was watching the TV with me and I was watching it alone. I was moving around meeting all of the Simpsons' family.

I was putting a big fat clown suit on as I remembered I was wearing big, thick, sweaty wellington boots. I was fighting with Marge and Maggie because I was frightened. My heart started to beat faster and faster until I could hear it. I was on the floor screaming to get out.

I woke up and I had doctors and nurses crowded around me. I didn't know what was happening so I asked my mum and she said, 'You've been knocked out for two whole hours.'

I had an excellent experience from that program and I will always remember that day.

Laura Ridley (10)
Greenland Junior School, Co Durham

Love's True Fall

There was once a girl called Jade who longed for a husband, and a boy called Jake who longed for a wife.

They saw each other from time to time but didn't pay much attention to one another, but one day Jake took a deep breath and went over to Jade when suddenly a boy with dark hair, swooped past him and kidnapped Jade!

He followed him and he led Jake to a wooden hut where Jade was put in a closet and locked in.

He snuck into the hut and Jake was also captured and put in there too.

Jade felt around and felt a switch so she turned it on and a light appeared.

Jake had seen an air vent above him, so they worked out a plan but it was dangerous. Just in case they didn't survive they kissed and they ran out of the hut and as soon as she got away Jade heard a gunshot and immediately she knew that Jake had died, then she cried and cried and cried.

As soon as she got home she informed the police and they arrested the man and recovered the body of Jake.

Jade was first to show up at the funeral.

When he was lowered into the grave, she threw roses into the grave and a bouquet of flowers too.

Depressed, Jade stabbed herself and fell in the grave to be close to Jake forever.

Ryan Purvis (10)
Greenland Junior School, Co Durham

The Strange Revenge Of Dr Donkin

One night when the moon was full I took a short cut to the shop. Behind a huge gravestone marked, 'Died in 1174' was the exit. I crept to the exit when a big, green, slimy hand lay on my shoulder, it was Shrek!

Shrek was a mean, green burping machine and it was disgusting how he ate snails' eyeballs. So we walked and walked and walked and walked until eventually we got out and there stood a thousand metre tall volcano.

'Let's climb it, it's safe, I think!'

Shrek started to climb, so I followed him.

At the top stood the superbly stupid, evil Dr Donkin.

'I had a feeling you would get here, Shrek!' he said.

'Any last words Donkin?' said Shrek.

'Yes please! Robo monkeys attack!'

As quick as a flash, Shrek pulled out a radio, *'Insania'* Peter Andre's dreadful singing blew up the monkeys.

Shrek was about to push Dr Donkin in the volcano but he said, 'Stop! Shrek I am your father.'

'You-you are?' mumbled Shrek.

Dr Donkin then said, 'No, but I love a happy ending don't you?'

'Oh shut up!' Shrek flicked him on the nose.

'Maaaammyy'

'I saved the world, I saved the world, er . . . *we* saved the world!' Shrek chanted happily.

Christopher Graham (9)
Greenland Junior School, Co Durham

Rain

I come . . . I go . . . it's the life for me. People shield themselves from me. All creatures great and small hide from me . . . arrgghh sunlight, it burns. It burns! I am gone, the world is spinning around me. Silly me I am back tomorrow when it all begins all over again.

Michael Hilton (11)
Holy Cross RC Primary School, North Tyneside

A Day In The Life Of An Evacuee

5th September 1939

I was up at 4.30 this morning thinking about my mother and father. I thought about what they would be doing at that precise moment. I then went back to sleep for another four hours.

When I woke up again I didn't think about my mother or father. I just got started doing my chores. I swept the floor of my tiny little bedroom, brushing all of the rats away. Next I went outside with the other evacuee children and fed the chickens, cows, horses, pigs and even the little fishes in the small pond. By this time it was breakfast time. It was bacon, toast, sausages and scrambled egg. I gobbled up every last crumb of toast, every last piece of scrambled egg and scraping of bacon and sausage. It was the second best breakfast in all the time I have lived.

Me and the other children went to our new school. It was very different to our old London school. We went through every single lesson without having to pack up and go into the Anderson shelter. We even went on a school trip to all of the shops, fields and even to see the head of the village Mr Covington. Mrs Hartrige, our teacher, showed us how to milk a cow. After school, she gave us each a large jug of the fresh flowing milk.

After we had drunk the milk, we all went home and we slept the night away.

Sally Grace Pentecost (9)
Hunwick Primary School, Co Durham

A Day In The Life Of An Evacuee

I woke up still shivering and then I went downstairs and ate my breakfast. It was porridge.

Then I went over to the school but it was very scary. The windows were gloomy and dark. The playground was dark but my teacher was a lot different than all of this, she was called Mrs Lamp.

I went into my class and there were rows of desks and a big one at the front for the teacher. Suddenly I saw the whip and the Dunce's cap.

I walked back home thinking about my family and wondering if they were okay. I just ran into the house and straight up to my bedroom. I looked at my family and I sat on my bed. Suddenly Mrs Apple called me for dinner, it was meat and potatoes. Maybe she enjoyed having me.

I went to look at the fish, they were golden and then I decided to go to bed.

Goodbye.

Laura Bradshaw (8)
Hunwick Primary School, Co Durham

A Day In The Life Of Henry VIII

I got up in the morning and had a great feast like I always do and it was one of the loveliest feasts I've ever had. After I went to practice some jousting and I won so I'm nearly at the top of the best list at jousting. I also thought I saw someone cheating! I absolutely hated that. After I went jousting again and I decided to do some beheading. It was so very disgusting. The best beheading I'd ever seen.

Soon after I went to find a new wife. I looked all over but I didn't find one that day though. So I walked up to some monks and started to terrorise them, the stupid things. It was one of my favourite things, terrorising monks. horribly. They ran away like the wind so I never saw them again. I looked for more women and I found the perfect one. I got her to like me a bit. I got her to marry me. I liked her so much that I I ordered that when I died I was to be buried next to her.

I needed a bit of practise with jousting for the finals. I practised with my wife's friend. For my favourite sport tennis, I had a little practise with my friend again. He looked like he cheated so I nearly ordered him to be beheaded. but I didn't want to behead my best friend. I had another practice at tennis and no one cheated, luckily; and the day finished.

Jack Liddell (9)
Hunwick Primary School, Co Durham

A Day In The Life Of An Evacuee

I was woken late at night by the air raid siren, I quickly put my dressing gown on and went into the shelter behind my foster house. I saw quite a few new animals. There was a cow, a pig, a dog and a rabbit. I then went to do some farming in the fields and went to play with the dog.

Later, I milked the cow and fed the pigs.

I emptied my bag, I had some things in my bag that you wouldn't have thought of, I had some cards, a lucky charm, a blanket, a picture of my friends and family and my little soft bear. I also had some things to eat like sandwiches and a cookie.

Sometimes I saw some bombers going overhead but not dropping bombs on us. They dropped them on the fields.

I had my dinner. We had fish and chips and I then went to the shop to get the newspaper for my foster parents. I managed to go home. I went to see my friends and we then went out for tea. We had some food from the corner shop and some of it was warm. It was then getting dark so my friend went home and I listened to the radio then I put on my pyjamas, had some supper and I felt tired so I went upstairs to get into bed. But before bed, I thought of all the things I had done that day.

Christopher Housecroft (10)
Hunwick Primary School, Co Durham

A Day In The Life Of Henry VIII

I woke up at 7 o'clock this morning and had my breakfast. Later through the day I went to play tennis, then I went jousting and I won every time. After that I went hunting and I managed to get loads of rabbits and then I went to spend some time with my wife, Anne Boleyn. Then I went to talk to my employee for a while.

I went dancing at the dancing hall, it was really good. Sometimes my wife comes and I dance with her, we do disco dancing, old-fashioned dancing, some people show the rest of the class what they're dancing is like.

Then we had the feast, it was really good.

Megan Maddison (9)
Hunwick Primary School, Co Durham

A Day In The Life Of An Evacuee

I was woken up this morning by a really loud noise.

My mum put me on the nearest train, I was excited and scared at the same time because I'd never been on a train before and I was scared because I would be by myself and I would miss my family. When I was on the train, it was really fun. When I got to the countryside, it was really early so I had breakfast, it was lovely, I had bacon, sausage, egg and fried bread. A bit later we went to the shop and I bought a new bike, well the person who I was staying with bought it for me. She is really nice to me and she has her own children, who I can play with. They had bikes too. Then we had dinner, it was yummy but not as yummy as breakfast, I had beans and sausage on toast.

After that we went to a farm and we were milking cows and picking strawberries and potatoes. When we got back we went down the river on our bikes. It was really fun. We went back home and had tea and now I'm writing in my diary.

Nicole Green (10)
Hunwick Primary School, Co Durham

A Day In The Life Of An Evacuee

I have to get up at six o'clock in the morning to get my bacon and eggs, because I have to help Mr Miller milk the cows. Mr Miller is the man who I'm staying with, so I got my breakfast then went outside to help him.

When I got outside, his dog came running towards me. I tried to find the cow shed so I looked round and then I saw a cow, so I ran to Mr Miller who shouted to the dog. It ran away and we started to milk the cows. Mr Miller showed me how to milk a cow.

After we had milked all of the cows, (which took three hours to do) I turned hungry, so I asked Mr Miller if we could get some food. He said we had to wait until we got the hens done, then we could eat the free range eggs. I asked him what free range eggs were and he said, 'They're when hens go free range, that means they are allowed to walk wherever they want to.'

So I started to collect the eggs. We collected 53 eggs and decided to have egg and chips. I dipped all of my chips into my egg it was gorgeous. After my tea, I went to bed.

Richard James (9)
Hunwick Primary School, Co Durham

A Day In The Life Of J K Rowling

Right, today I got up and got ready and while I was eating my breakfast, you know what I did? Yes, I wrote another chapter of my sixth Harry Potter book 'The Half-Blood Prince'.

About an hour later, I went to sign some autographs. Soon after, my mother came to take me home in her massive limo. Signing some more autographs my hand started to ache.

'Oh darling, your hands are all red. Take a break,' said Mrs Rowling.

'Okay Mum, I'll take a break,' I said painfully. But I never did, I carried on writing my new book. It was very detailed, I think it should be finished in about a few months.

After that I went in my swimming pool. My mother came along, 'Oh very good, you're chilling out,' my mum said. Then I fell asleep in the pool and that is a day in the life of me - J K Rowling.

Jamie Campbell (9)
Hunwick Primary School, Co Durham

A Day In The Life Of A Thoroughbred

I went into my stable and my owner came and gave me some Polos. Mmm, I love Polos. After that I lay down for a nap, but my owner woke me up and said, 'Dash, come on let's go in the field.'

So he led me on to my juicy green grass, there he left me so I ran over to Goly my best friend, he was with Whisper and Tobey. We were playing with the water jump. We were jumping over it.

My owner shouted to me again, 'Dash, Dash come on!' He had Polos in his hand.

I ran to him, he put me in my stable and went to get my tack. I got tacked up for a little girl to ride me. I went into a trot and a canter. I jumped over a jump for one metre and a half, then stopped.

Mark got on me and he went over a jump, two metres and a hole, I nearly tripped and fell. I skidded on the sand and I nearly fell again.

He took me back into my stable and fed me Polos again. I will never get sick of Polos because they are scrumptious.

I stamped on Mark's foot while he was getting my tack off. He took me out to the field to sleep.

Ellie Pryce (10)
Hunwick Primary School, Co Durham

What's That Coming?

I'm in a gloomy situation on my own. What should I do? I am gripping onto the walls, ready to sprint, because I know something's going to come. My hands sweat. What's that coming? Should I dash or should I stay? If it finds me what will it say?

Amy Jury (11)
Kelloe Primary School, Co Durham

Awake At Night

Whirr . . . whirr . . . squeeeeaaak, round and round, getting louder and louder. I wondered if it would ever stop. It was really getting on my nerves. I felt exhausted. It stopped. I was nearly asleep but it started again . . . *whirr.* He keeps me awake . . . my pet mouse Stuart in his wheel.

Rosie Craggs (11)
Kelloe Primary School, Co Durham

Bridges

I felt the rumbling in my belly, the banging in my head. I felt the thud of footsteps, the creak of the floor, I felt like I was going to fall. The trees, bushes, rails and creatures came closer and closer.

I stepped off the bridge, safe at last.

Laura Williams (10)
Kelloe Primary School, Co Durham

Help Me!

I see the stars gleaming into the sky. The moon hanging next to me. I take a peak down to the ground. My heart is thudding like a drum. People watch me from down below. My heart is normal now. At last I'm down.

Emma Turton (10)
Kelloe Primary School, Co Durham

Hare Coursing

I am watching the course, it is amazing. My head is spinning round and round. My heart is thud, thud, thudding. I am filling up with excitement. I am ready to scream and shout. The dog is getting closer and closer, faster and faster. Finally the dog caught the hare.

Colin Hall (11)
Kelloe Primary School, Co Durham

Never Again

My heart thuds. My hair blows. I'm going to be sick. Get me off this thing, stop it. I want to scream but no sound comes out. I grip on to the bar. Aarrgghh! My hands sweat, my hairs stand up on end. No more roller coasters for me.

Shannon Richardson (11)
Kelloe Primary School, Co Durham

Heights

Thoughts leapt into my brain, *what if I fall? What if I break a bone?* My life flashed before my eyes when suddenly a pair of arms grabbed me. 'Heeelp!' I yelled as I got lowered to the floor. I really, really, *really* hate heights.

Samantha Dobson (11)
Kelloe Primary School, Co Durham

No More For Me

'Argh! Argh! Slow down you're going too fast.' This animal is rapid. It is as fierce as a lion and is as fast as a car. 'Slow down man, slow down.' That's why you shouldn't jump on a cheetah's back. It is terrifying. No more for me.

Daley Hetherington (11)
Kelloe Primary School, Co Durham

Go-Karting

I felt my breath reflecting off the helmet. I couldn't see, my breath was fogging the screen. I could just see the road. I could feel the heat of the engine beside me. I could see the wheels spinning as I flew against the finish line and chequered flag.

Carl Hill (11)
Kelloe Primary School, Co Durham

The Jungle

I was in the jungle and a tiger came up behind me. I shouted, 'No-no-no!' My heart was pounding. Shivers were crawling up my spine, I was paralysed. *Bang!* A gun exploded close by. The tiger fled away! I was safe.

Matthew Daley (11)
Kelloe Primary School, Co Durham

Help!

A frightened feeling jumped into my stomach as I was pulled forward. All I could hear was the thud, thud of my heart. Suddenly I went dizzy. I thought I was going to faint. Bushes, trees, fences all spinning round and round. Help! That's why I hate horse riding.

Jessica Taylor (9)
Kelloe Primary School, Co Durham

The Magical Dream

There I was standing in front of an extraordinary machine. A frozen swirl of air twirled round me making me dizzy and sick. I felt as if I was floating higher and higher into the sky. Birds and trees whizzed past me. That's why I really hate aeroplanes.

Bethany Morrow (9)
Kelloe Primary School, Co Durham

The Magic Tunnel

There I was standing outside of the tunnel, suddenly something wrapped round my leg pulling me into the dusty tunnel. I got up. A train was coming speeding down. I couldn't move because the bright light was shining in my eyes. Argh! I woke up, it was all a dream.

Nicola Potts (10)
Kelloe Primary School, Co Durham

Haunted

He rushed through the crooked floors. He just could not help feeling petrified, scared and alone, but he soon realised that he wasn't. The floorboards creaked and then he knew he was not alone. He was going furiously down the passageway, then he heard a noise. It's over!

Robert Crawford (10)
Kelloe Primary School, Co Durham

World War X

Bang! The troops withdrew, it was too powerful.
   'My leg is injured!'
   The army was weak. No one stood a chance.
   'Argh!'
   'Help me!'
   The feeling was like drowning in pools of death. I was in pain as if I was melting. Then I stopped! Look it's Van Helsing.
   'Yeah!'

Liam Simpson (10)
Kelloe Primary School, Co Durham

Seeing Stars

My heart pounded as I whooshed away. I peered out a minute window. All I knew was that I was speeding. But I had a fishy feeling about this. It didn't feel like I was going along. It felt like I was going up. I realised I was seeing stars!

Laura Jones (9)
Kelloe Primary School, Co Durham

Mini Saga

His arms started to shake. His heart started to tremble as he ran further and further into the woods. He did not notice the monstrous beast with rotten teeth and endless spikes on his back all to go with his black heart. Then he awoke and whispered, 'I hate nightmares.'

Ruby Finley (9)
Kelloe Primary School, Co Durham

Cars Are Frightening

My heart was pounding. I could hear it thudding. My legs were wobbling. My stomach turned with thunder. I started to scream as a shiver ran down my spine. I rolled over with a fright as the car engine stopped. Oh, but I wish I was not afraid of cars.

Cara Thompson (9)
Kelloe Primary School, Co Durham

The Thing

There was a monstrous clash and someone yelled, 'Stampede!' They all scampered for their lives. The thing was chasing them. It was getting closer. They were petrified. Philip whispered, 'This cave is eerie.'

A voice said, 'Get out of my cave.'

'It's a mouse, wow. Let's keep it!'

Allan Jordan (10)
Kelloe Primary School, Co Durham

The Jungle

I snuck around the jungle with my enemy armed with potato guns looking for a rare parrot of Africa. Suddenly there's a noise, it was *tat, tat*. I turned around and then I realised I wasn't in the jungle. I was in a potato field looking for a woodpecker!

Philip Jones (10)
Kelloe Primary School, Co Durham

Roller Coasters

He got pulled in by something. It trapped him to a chair. Help, it was spinning round and round. Help, it was spinning faster and faster, help. And gosh, his glasses smashed, he had terrible cuts on his face and that's why he hates roller coasters so very, very much.

Jade Templeton (10)
Kelloe Primary School, Co Durham

Hunters

I'm in the jungle. Some hunters are there too. They set up camp, guns in their bags along with knives and bullets. I sneak in the van, cheetahs and tigers all dead. I feel drowsy, my body drops as they come. I am captured. I've been daydreaming, silly me.

Samantha Hill (9)
Kelloe Primary School, Co Durham

The Dark Mines

The mines are dark and damp. Candles flicker, chisels bang on the wall, puddles splash when people trudge through. Explosions in the distance. Pushing the trains on the track, the men coughing and spluttering. Rocks fall from the wall.

Edward Kidd (8)
Langwathby CE Primary School, Cumbria

Down The Mine

Here I am standing on the crystal rock. I hear banging and explosions. Candles are burning and shadows are flickering. The horses are clanking loudly. There are men shouting loudly. Stones fall on people's heads.

Cameron Harvey (8)
Langwathby CE Primary School, Cumbria

A Viking Saga

The sea roared and the sky was devil-red. The angry sea serpent slithered towards me, a jolt of frightening energy flowed through me like a rushing river. The stars twinkled and the moon shone like diamonds. The great leap of the enormous sea serpent crushed the boat and me.

Bradley Neen (9)
Langwathby CE Primary School, Cumbria

Football Saga

My feet were trembling as Ricardo ambled up to take the penalty. The crowd roared and chanted as I tightened my gloves and peered at the name David James. Ricardo tried to flatten the mashed up penalty spot, lay the ball on the grass, he took it, I dived, goal.

James Sharp (9)
Langwathby CE Primary School, Cumbria

Storm!

The sky was as black as velvet, the stars like diamonds. I was sailing across the Black Sea. The waves sprayed water in my face. Then I realised I would never ride a longship again. Suddenly a massive wave hurled over the boat and I got swept overboard.

Lauren Snowball (9)
Langwathby CE Primary School, Cumbria

A Viking Saga

The sky was black with stars as bright as the sun, it looked like a wizard's cloak, the wind blew and the sea crashed on the rocks. What was happening? The witches cackled above us like they had just made the storm worse.

Megan Wilson (9)
Langwathby CE Primary School, Cumbria

Sick Boat

Here we are on the battleship. The sea is crashing against us. It feels like I am sitting side saddle on a rocking horse. *Swish,* I've been splashed fifty-four times now. My hair is soaking and a horrendous storm is approaching. We better get under cover quick!

Isobel Everatt (8)
Langwathby CE Primary School, Cumbria

The Dark Mines

The mines are dark. I can't feel my fingers. I'm shaking, shivering. My feet are icy cold. It's dark and damp. Candles flashing in the water rushing beside the track. Hammers bashing together. Rocks falling, water splashing. Feet trudging about. People running, slipping and hurting themselves. People screaming, yelling, shouting.

Tom Holme (8)
Langwathby CE Primary School, Cumbria

Sudden Changes

It was a beautiful day, we slowly sped southward from Sweden. The sky turned black as velvet. Thor got angry, lightning came down like a stone in water. It sliced off the figurehead which stuck to the mast, it turned into a dragon. It came down . . . I went blank.

Harry Leah (8)
Langwathby CE Primary School, Cumbria

The Mine

One wet day I go down the mine. It is my first day. All I can hear is gunpowder banging, rats squeaking, horses trotting, people running, people chatting, helmets crashing, carts rolling, water falling, stones bashing, boxes smashing. I can see shiny stones in my eyes.

Donald Burrow (9)
Langwathby CE Primary School, Cumbria

Misty, Gloomy Mine

I stand hearing trickling water, the tap, tap, tap of the pickaxes, the clank of carriages being hauled, the rumble of ore being tipped, the slow clip-clop of hooves trudging, voices silent.

Here I stand in the dull, cold, misty mine with water trickling down in the gaps of the mine. I work with the horses trudging by my side. I feel sad, scared and lonely. There is no light in the misty, gloomy mine.

Holly Streatfield (8)
Langwathby CE Primary School, Cumbria

Down In The Lead Mine

Down in the lead mine, where the noises of the horse and carts echo through the mine, I hear the trickling of the water as it soaks through the ground and the chip, chop of pickaxes. The golden flicker of the candlelight lights my way safely home.

Ellen Greenop (8)
Langwathby CE Primary School, Cumbria

A Viking Saga

I was trembling all over, I could smell smoke, I could feel the heat. I started to cry but then I heard a voice that I recognised, my mother! She was crying as well. I soon found out why. Elfreda, my sister, had been killed. Father had been killed as well.

Megan Liddle (8)
Langwathby CE Primary School, Cumbria

Black Night

The sky is as black as space on a Monday night. When the stars shone down to Earth the Vikings set off on their stormy journey to find some treasures. The boat was rocking from side to side while the waves were twisting like some curly hair amongst the sea.

Alice Sandells (8)
Langwathby CE Primary School, Cumbria

Black Velvet Boat

Black sky covered the heavens like black velvet. The waves were lofty and they went over the ship. It was difficult to steer the boat and my feet were trembling and my hands were quivering. I had no food and had been travelling for one moon, my travellers had died.

Rebecca Didcock (8)
Langwathby CE Primary School, Cumbria

The Vikings' Invasion

I am a Saxon boy in Langwathby. A Viking raid is upon us. We are getting ready to battle. 'Get ready,' we say, 'the Vikings are just coming the hill.' We fire the first line of arrows, they get nearer and nearer but we kill the first 100 Vikings.

Jonathan Crisp (8)
Langwathby CE Primary School, Cumbria

The Monster

I stepped inside the feared place and closed the door. I felt a shiver run down my spine. I crept up to the entrance. I called out, 'Hello! Is anybody in here?' It echoed. I opened the door and screamed, *'Argh! It's hideous!'* I heard my mother's voice. 'The cheek!'

Aiden Goulden (10)
St Mary's Meadowside Primary School, Sunderland

Fear . . .

I've always been petrified. They were there concealing me in their jet-black bodies.

I lay there, cold sweat covering every inch of my body. And the only message my brain was sending to me was fear.

I wished that I wasn't scared of spiders. I've never slept since.

Christie Bainbridge (10)
St Mary's Meadowside Primary School, Sunderland

The Skeleton

I heard a scream from down the corridor. What could it be? Nerves were tingling down my spine. My legs were stiff, I couldn't move. Something was coming towards me. 'Help, help,' I cried. It lifted its arms up and took its cloak off. I couldn't bear to look.

William Lewis (9)
St Mary's Meadowside Primary School, Sunderland

Night-Time Terror

I was walking with my friend, there was something following us. It was getting closer. My heart was beating really quick. My friend tripped over. The dinosaur was coming. We ran and ran but . . . the dinosaur got us.

Melanie Golding (10)
St Mary's Meadowside Primary School, Sunderland

The Dream

I always wondered if my dreams were real. Whatever I dreamt of came true. I didn't dream anything good, like getting rich and winning the lottery. I told my friends, but they thought I was joking. Mrs Fate, the fortune teller was the only one who believed me. *That* was no help. She's as nutty as a mixed bag of fruit and nuts without the fruit.

But last night, I had a dream. Even though I only had the dream yesterday, I still can't remember most of it. I'll tell you what I know.

It was as if the world had gone black. I could hear screaming, groaning. I screamed and yelled too, but no one came . . .

Then I woke up, a cold sweat all over me. I was gasping for air.

Today I went to see Mrs Fate and asked her about it. She gasped and said in her misty, faraway voice, 'My goodness! You must come to see me tomorrow! I'll tell you everything!'

So there it is. I'm going to go and see her tomorrow, to see what it meant. Mrs Fate might be strange . . . but she might have answers too . . .

Ashleigh Simpson (10)
St Mary's Meadowside Primary School, Sunderland

Mini Saga

I felt like I was bleeding running from the horn-headed man. The sweat was dropping down my head, you could count a litre of water in it. My legs felt like they were going to fall off from all the moving. I was relieved when I woke up.

Matthew Wake (10)
St Mary's Meadowside Primary School, Sunderland

Scaredy-Cat

I stood shaking on a bumpy rock, not wanting to move while I could hear tinkling metal. My stomach trembled, my bones wobbled. Looking down, I felt a hundred metres off the ground, I jumped off a climbing frame, safely on the floor I stood. I'm afraid of heights!

Caitlin Hindmarsh (9)
St Mary's Meadowside Primary School, Sunderland

Before I Fall

I stand up there before I fall, get me down don't let me die. Standing there seeing the ground. Trying not to fall. I keep a good grip as I try to get down. A lump grows in my throat, I can't move. I'm terrified, it's my fear of heights.

Georgina Currie (10)
St Mary's Meadowside Primary School, Sunderland

Terror!

I heard my mother screaming with pain from the knife that was held by the murderer with blood dripping down from it. I stood there watching. I opened my mouth to scream but nothing came out of it. My mother lay there not breathing and not moving. She was dead.

Emily Bird (10)
St Mary's Meadowside Primary School, Sunderland

My One True Passion

It's my one true love, I couldn't live without it. Nobody can compare to its pure soft side, it's heavenly. I take it to work every day. I'd sacrifice my home for it. It's oh so lovely inside, so rich and fine. I just love chocolate, it's oh so sweet.

Jessica Pye (10)
St Mary's Meadowside Primary School, Sunderland

Argh!

My whole body trembled, I took a wobbly step back. Sweat ran down the back of neck. I felt my friend, she was shaking from head to foot. I was terrified. The bushes moved again. Were we surrounded? The bush lurched . . . Argh! The deadly *T-rex* was after us!

Sarah Forrest (10)
St Mary's Meadowside Primary School, Sunderland

A Night-Time Scare

As I travelled up the stairs, with the light gleaming before me I heard footsteps below me, something was following me up the stairs! I couldn't look down, I was too scared. I started to run, the footsteps got faster. I looked down and realised they were mine!

Rebecca Smith (10)
St Mary's Meadowside Primary School, Sunderland

The Kamakazi

I slid down, it grew darker and darker. Sweat dribbled down my back, I began to feel cold. My back skipped off the surface, I flew up in the air, I could feel goosebumps rising like mini volcanoes on my skin. I flew into the water, the slide was great.

Anthony Callaghan (10)
St Mary's Meadowside Primary School, Sunderland

The Slide

I could hardly speak I was so nervous. I gently stepped up on to the first rung of the ladder, my feet were like jelly as they splashed sharply. I began to step to the last rung. I slowly closed my eyes and felt like it was my worst nightmare.

Luke Gibbins (10)
St Mary's Meadowside Primary School, Sunderland

Roller Coasters

Sweat ran down from my forehead, I was breathing heavily. I felt sick and scared, I was about to cry. I covered my eyes as I hurtled forward, eventually it slowed down. I opened my eyes, we had stopped, I hate roller coasters!

Katherine Lamb (10)
St Mary's Meadowside Primary School, Sunderland

The Terrible Train

My heart thumped like a fist on the table. It was screeching like a cave of bats. All eyes were glaring out like a dead body. Light came in as the jet-black doors opened. I stepped out; I will never go on a train again.

Craig MacDonald (10)
St Mary's Meadowside Primary School, Sunderland

Plane

The hairs on my neck and back stood up on end. I was shaking like mad! My feet could barely go in front of each other. The steps were like a pyramid. Cold sweat ran down my face, I felt hot and uncomfortable. My fear of planes will never go!

Melissa Quinn (10)
St Mary's Meadowside Primary School, Sunderland

In The Lift

I felt hot and uncomfortable. Sweat ran down my face. The hairs on my arms stood up. I began to shake all over. We started to fall. Now there was no turning back. I shut my eyes firmly and wished, really wished that I didn't have to travel in lifts.

Eszter Soos (10)
St Mary's Meadowside Primary School, Sunderland

Euro 2004 Semi

I wanted the Portuguese to get beaten but they won 2-1. Then it was the Czech Republic's chance to beat Greece. I wished that I was Pavel Nedved and it came true!

I was just getting ready for kick-off. We kicked off and I had the ball, I passed back to Poborsky then Poborsky passed it to Baros, then he did a long ball up the pitch to me. Then I passed it to Koller, then he had a shot and forced a fantastic save by Nikopolidos. Then Greece got on the attack and Giankoupoulos passed to Charisteas, he had a shot and it hit the bar. I got the ball and I started running, then I reached the edge of the box and I shot but it went wide. It was now the 39th minute and the Czechs were playing the best, Baros missed a sitter.

It was now half-time and everyone on the team was talking about Baros' sitter miss. Our manager was telling us that we were the best team on the pitch. There were 5 minutes into the second half and the Greeks hit the bar. Then I got the ball and passed it to Poborsky and Baros scored but it was offside. It was now the 73rd minute and there was nothing much happening. It was extra time and they scored. 1-0 to Greece.

Mark Middleton (10)
St Mary's Meadowside Primary School, Sunderland

The Road To Hell

Every Hallowe'en a sacred creature arises from Hell and the cursed house that covers the gateway. All the mysterious monsters protect the house so that no great hero can defeat the mighty Grim Reaper, along with his dreaded companions. Not for three thousand years has anyone killed a Grim Reaper. The legendary Grim Reaper has a deadly attack with his unbreakable slicing axe. And now his magic slave casts dreading fireballs all over the world bringing pain and suffering to all.

He orders his pets, the alien and the goblin, to torture and kill people. This will keep happening until a brave warrior with the most strength and pure of heart can have the courage to kill the Grim Reaper. What makes a man a man? Is it his wits? No! It's his bravery against the most appalling enemies. But the hero in this story is called Hellboy and alone he will win the world its freedom.

As he enters the enemies' ground he grows scared but when he sees his enemy he grows fierce and is determined to kill the Grim Reaper. However, all of the gravestones were putting him near his opponent. His magician took out the sword of justice and gave it to his master, but it was no use against a man with mostly strength and pure of heart, so he was vanquished back to Hell and was not allowed out.

Daniel Pinchen (10)
St Mary's Meadowside Primary School, Sunderland

Tomb

I steadily walked through. Sweat gathered in the palms of my hands, my tummy churned. Hairs stood up on the back of my neck. I got to the point where my legs trembled, my teeth chattered. I dropped the torch and ran to the next level of the tomb.

Josie Barlow (10)
St Mary's Meadowside Primary School, Sunderland

A Sax To Remember

It was so lonely because everyone else was asleep so I put on my raincoat and wandered out into the darkness with my saxophone. Everything was a blur in the darkness. I staggered over to the old tree house and played a melody, the tune echoed through the caravan park.

Paige Gilbert (10)
St Mary's Meadowside Primary School, Sunderland

Fear

There I was, my hands curling, my tummy lurching. It was getting closer and closer until its tail smacked me like someone had punched me in the tummy. I shouted, I called, I screamed but no one came. It turned round and went. I wish I wasn't scared of sharks.

Olivia Newby (10)
St Mary's Meadowside Primary School, Sunderland

Through The Tunnel

At the end of the tunnel you hear the clack of metal on the stone floor, you hear people talking, you hear roars and cheers from the other end of the tunnel. You hear a sort of musical introduction. We leave the tunnel and run onto the football pitch.

Cameron Phillips (10)
St Mary's Meadowside Primary School, Sunderland

Darkness

My teeth shivered, my face dropped. I felt a sudden crawl of a tarantula. I stepped away, I was really, really scared. It was pitch-black. It was as dark as millions of white cats tossed in oil, as deep as the sea, until the light came on.

Elliot Harris (9)
St Mary's RC Primary School, Newcastle upon Tyne

A Day In The Life Of Beth Wilkinson

My face felt droopy, my eyes were watery and I was shivering. It felt horrible as I was hanging onto the bridge with only one arm. I tried to pull myself up but it was too hard, what on earth could I do? It was dreadful.

Suddenly my hand slipped and I fell off! Argh! But then when I landed I didn't feel a thing. All that I felt was something going inside my nose. Then I looked and I saw that I'd landed in some horse's hay. Then the owner of the horse came to me and said, 'Would you like some help?' Then he carried me home.

Beth Wilkinson (9)
St Mary's RC Primary School, Newcastle upon Tyne

Spiders

I am so afraid of spiders, they creep right down my neck. They're creepy and scary beasts. I tell you now don't go near one. Don't go near those beasts they're scary, creepy creatures. 'What on earth shall I do? There's one right there - shall I stand on it?'

'No!'

Mairead Hunt (9)
St Mary's RC Primary School, Newcastle upon Tyne

A Day In The Life Of Delta Goodrum

I woke with a start. My alarm was going off and it was 6am. (As usual.)

I felt a sharp pain. It was okay though, I had learned to live with it. Since I was diagnosed with Hodgkin's Disease, I was used to these. My music and acting careers were put on hold but I kept on with my song writing. Everyone called me a fighter. I knew I had to get back to my careers before I was a tiny spot in people's minds. I'm on my way to a full recovery now.

Anyway, Delta stop babbling. As most people know I am working hard on my second album. There are times I just don't know what to do, but at the minute I am going to get dressed and have breakfast.

I am travelling to the studio in a van. I love the studio, it's my second home, I spend so much time there!

I am now at the studio. I have to record songs for my second album. I am allowed dinner with my friends in town, as long as I'm back by 1pm. I'm back in the studio from lunch and am working on some more songs. I clock off at 5pm so until then I've got to sing.

It has been and gone 5pm. I'm at home now. I sometimes go out with my friends after work. I couldn't be bothered tonight. I was so tired after singing my heart out. Goodnight. With love, Delta.

Rachael Bell (11)
St Mary's RC Primary School, Newcastle upon Tyne

A Mini Saga

There I was getting on the most horrifying thing in the world. Suddenly, I got in. It started. Argh! Argh! Argh! I felt like I was going to crash. The worst thing that could happen to me happened, I fell. Argh! Argh! Argh! I fell out of a *boat*.

Stephanie Saxelby (9)
St Mary's RC Primary School, Newcastle upon Tyne

A Mini Saga

I just hate it. I'm up a million feet, scared. People wanting me to do it. I place my legs on the huge blue ramp. I can't do it. I put my hands on the side and push . . . I'm going 100mph! I've done it! I'm not afraid of slides!

Calum Sordy (9)
St Mary's RC Primary School, Newcastle upon Tyne

A Mini Saga

I hate slugs, they creep up my back. When I pick up a stone I quickly put it down because they are everywhere especially under stones. They are slimy and gooey. They always will be. They are a mortal enemy to me. Their back hasn't a hard, strong shell.

Isabella Mercer Jones (8)
St Mary's RC Primary School, Newcastle upon Tyne

Death Of A Bum

The great white bum was powerful, but not powerful enough for the korpido blaster. Zack fired the bumcano and shot the bum too, then the bumcano while it was rattling. The bumcano shot him into space and through a brown hole. He screamed and was killed on Uranus!

Daragh Rogerson (9)
St Mary's RC Primary School, Newcastle upon Tyne

Mini Saga

There it was jiggling about, ready to come out! Sitting, saying, It's coming!' I warned. 'B . . . b . . . b . . . bleurgh!' It came, and yuck, what a stink! All over, the car. I should have used the bag or out the window. Actually not the window, but it had to be in the car!

Jack Thompson (9)
St Mary's RC Primary School, Newcastle upon Tyne

A Mini Saga

I dreamt I was sitting while witches made their potions. Sweat dripping down my body, hotness drifting onto my face as I sat quietly in the chair. They walked over slowly and I moved further back. I drank the potion they gave me and closed my eyes. That's strange!

Emily Norman (9)
St Mary's RC Primary School, Newcastle upon Tyne

Mini Saga

I was standing in the shed trembling with fear, screaming in my head. I couldn't walk. I was so terrified. I wasn't even concentrating on what I was looking at. Suddenly I screamed without noticing, 'Hhheeelllppp!' This made it shudder and climb back up.

At last I revealed it, 'Spider!'

Sarah Boyd (9)
St Mary's RC Primary School, Newcastle upon Tyne

Seasick

I began to feel queasy, my tummy wobbled about and my cheeks went bulgy, I think it's coming out. My body went up and down and my ears ached, it's that noise. My heart almost skipped a beat or two. Ow, how I don't like being seasick.

Daniel Tiffin (8)
Shincliffe CE Primary School, Co Durham

My Scary Day

I once was getting on a helicopter, I was so scared I couldn't touch it a single bit! My legs were shivering as I stepped forward to get in the helicopter. I was so scared of the propellers. I went in and closed my eyes and . . . it was lovely!

Emma Farman (8)
Shincliffe CE Primary School, Co Durham

What Life Is All About

It was dark and creepy. Everything was slimy. It was warm though. I froze. My heart was beating fast. Suddenly . . . I saw light. I got pulled down and it was not wet. How could I be afraid of coming into real life with Mum!

Louise Carnaby (8)
Shincliffe CE Primary School, Co Durham

My Fear Of Trains!

My hands were sweating as I jiggered up and down, it felt like my tummy turned inside out, and my teeth were chattering. I skidded down the pathway and landed on somebody's knee! They slapped me hard! I wished I hadn't got a fear of trains!

Lucy Kirkup (8)
Shincliffe CE Primary School, Co Durham

A Big Fear Of Spiders

As I was walking down some creepy wooden stairs I saw a . . . big, hairy, brown tarantula! It was getting closer to me. I felt like screaming but I was the only person in this building. Then I realised I was controlling the spider and the spider was fake!

Oliver Hobson (7)
Shincliffe CE Primary School, Co Durham

Fear

I saw the Devil, an evil pure red skin colour with slow moving molten lava all around him, he had a red fire fisherman's spear in his hand. He had evil piercing eyes as if they were spears. I wish I was not scared of the cinema!

Robert Blalek (8)
Shincliffe CE Primary School, Co Durham

My Fear

My body started to tingle and I started to sweat then my legs went stiff. Suddenly I stopped because my tummy went funny, then I screamed and fell on the floor. In one second I got up and noticed that I was in an aeroplane.

Elliot Kay (8)
Shincliffe CE Primary School, Co Durham

Fear Of Firsts

I jumped out of my skin. 'Help me!' I said. My mum pushed my dreaded body down the path. I tried to run but the bushes were in the way! I banged my head on the fence. 'Oww!' I wailed. I wished I didn't have such a fear of school.

Felix Dayan (7)
Shincliffe CE Primary School, Co Durham

The Fire

As smoke rose up into the sky a lot of sweat dribbled down my back. The smoke got higher. I backed off away from the smoke and the fire burnt away. It looked like a devil of death. I hate being me because I am afraid of barbecues.

Ewan Hill (8)
Shincliffe CE Primary School, Co Durham

Roller Coaster

My hands sweat with fear as we went round and then up . . . I was terrified. We had stopped! Time for the drop! Off we went. I closed my eyes and thought, *only three more dips to go.* We stopped. I got off and looked at the roller coaster. Never again.

Alison Laing (8)
Shincliffe CE Primary School, Co Durham

The Planet

One Monday morning I seemed to have woken up on a strange planet. Luckily I was wearing a spacesuit. I started to jump over to a big crater, it started to rumble so I took a step back and it exploded. What was that I saw in the distance?

Emma Callaghan (8)
Shincliffe CE Primary School, Co Durham

Find The Peg

Under the sofa, under the sink, where is the peg? It felt like my nose was blocked and I couldn't talk. In the cupboard, under the bed I still can't find it. Erggg where can it be? I wipe my face with my hands. The peg, clipped to my nose!

Olivia Karnacz (8)
Shincliffe CE Primary School, Co Durham

Where Are My Glasses

'Argh! Mum where are my glasses!' I shouted. 'They are my best ones.' My legs started to shake, I needed them for school! 'My teacher will give me detention if I don't have them for school!' Then suddenly I felt something tickling in my hair. They were in my hair!

Gemma Morgan (8)
Shincliffe CE Primary School, Co Durham

The Dark Room

Sweat was gently dripping down the back of my neck. I felt scared as my throat grew tighter. I shivered with fright. I shouted for my mummy. She said, 'Just go to bed.'

I said, 'I'm scared of the . . . *dark!*'

Rebecca Lambert (8)
Shincliffe CE Primary School, Co Durham

In The Desert!

Phew! At last something to drink. First to check I'll sip a bit then I'll drink. 'Cough, cough!' Fearfully I fell to the floor. I knew I should not have drunk it, then suddenly . . . I realised it was only water. 'Ha, ha, ha, ha!'

Mae Cuthbertson (7)
Shincliffe CE Primary School, Co Durham

Cardiff

My legs trembled as I walked backwards. I stared straight ahead, sweating like mad in the scorching sunlight. My heart was beating wildly. I felt like every eye in Britain was watching me do this. I ran at full speed, hoping to score from the spot . . .

Jason Jones (8)
Shincliffe CE Primary School, Co Durham

Big Foot

In the prehistoric jungle Big Foot was lurking in the bushes. I crept behind the tree and froze. Big Foot growled loudly and my stomach lurched as he pulled the bush out of the ground and when I saw him I ran out of the clearing and out of sight . . .

David Mitchell (8)
Shincliffe CE Primary School, Co Durham

Abseiling Fear

When I got up there my hands started to sweat. Suddenly I started to shiver. I climbed over the top, I was really scared. I started to feel nervous, I felt as if I had a group of spiders crawling up my back from the fear of abseiling! Argh!

Kate Wood (8)
Shincliffe CE Primary School, Co Durham

My Dad Snores

My legs were shaking like mad, I didn't know what it was so I just left it and kept behind the chair. Then I heard *zzzzzzz* - I had to poke Dad, because if I didn't I would still be terrified. Why am I scared of Dad's snoring?

Gabrielle Latcham (8)
Shincliffe CE Primary School, Co Durham

War Room

The thundering of bullets filled the room. 300 people, how many left? Screams of the wounded, blood of the dead, then as the sky turned black the roaring bullets stopped. My sister woke me up, although, it felt so real and I still had scars to prove it!

Nathan Finlay (10)
Swalwell Primary School, Newcastle upon Tyne

Cave Fear

Sweat dripped off my face as I ventured further into the gloom. Fear had a hold of me as I left the light of the beach behind. But I got the fright of my life when a corner blocked out the light and I was suspended in total darkness.

James Gillender (10)
Swalwell Primary School, Newcastle upon Tyne

The Wild, Wild West

I was tied to it, too tight. I struggled a lot, I couldn't break free, yes! The rope was coming slack. I heard the train rushing along at speed. I broke free with 10 seconds to spare, then the train came. I dived into the path of the train. *Splat!*

Gary Boyd (11)
Swalwell Primary School, Newcastle upon Tyne

The Cat

There it was standing on top of the bin. I told it to go away. Soon after it jumped on the fence. Extraordinarily it disappeared, what happened to that strange, odd, unusual, peculiar, remarkable, queer, unknown, different, dull, weird, small thing? Did it want food, that silly cat?

Vanessa Pears (9)
Swalwell Primary School, Newcastle upon Tyne

Ride On A Coaster

Sweat dripping, panic rushing, girls screaming. Speeding along the tracks like never before, loop to loop, side to side. Aarrgghh! I dropped from the tracks. Death was coming closer, closer, almost here. It was here, the last breath that anyone heard from me was . . . help!

David McGee (11)
Swalwell Primary School, Newcastle upon Tyne

The Jungle

I walked into the forest hoping that I would get home without being harmed. I was halfway through when I heard a rustling in the trees. I looked up, there was nothing there. Suddenly a claw ripped across my face.

'Argh! Mom the cat's spoiling my game!'

Shaun Kavanagh (11)
Swalwell Primary School, Newcastle upon Tyne

Splash

The storm battered the ship as the dreadful sea monster hurled gigantic waves at it. The mighty claw of the monster battered the top of the ship. A typhoon pulled the ship down. The plug was pulled. The baby was lifted out of the bath tub. The storm was over.

Leighton Wright (11)
Swalwell Primary School, Newcastle upon Tyne

Steven

It was too high. When I caught it it escaped, it was too swift. Higher and higher I jumped. Higher and higher it got, but still it was too high. I raised my net, swooped it for the last time and I caught it, it was a butterfly.

Steven Clark (11)
Swalwell Primary School, Newcastle upon Tyne

Running To Live

Running madly, like a dog chasing its tail. The brutal killer chasing him through the stony mountains, lurching on the sliding rocks. The rocks fell and he fell in a dinosaur's dark mouth. Then Johnny turned off his computer and slid into bed.

Danny Summerside (11)
Swalwell Primary School, Newcastle upon Tyne

Fear In The Darkness

Sweat ran down my palm not knowing what would happen next. I was terrified, suddenly the door slowly creaked. The whole bedroom was dark apart from a chink of light behind the door. I looked, suddenly a shadow appeared. I hid under the bed surrounded in darkness, something was appearing . . .

Connor Mullins (10)
Swalwell Primary School, Newcastle upon Tyne

A Different Planet

As time went by my legs shivered, sweat ran down my back. I realised I was on the planet Pluto. There were rocks that looked like stars and huge Martians. They looked like people but much bigger. They spotted me, my legs shivered even more. They spoke a different language.

Shannon White (9)
Swalwell Primary School, Newcastle upon Tyne

Death At A Drop

I was at the halfway point up the cliff. Near the top I had not much grip left, I had to hold on. I saw the faint figure of a person. What was it? I was scared. I did not move an inch. My fingers fell - aarrgghh!

James Wilson (11)
Swalwell Primary School, Newcastle upon Tyne

Never Again!

Muscles straining too hard to control. The power, I've never handled this before, it's outrageous, so strong. Pulled me forward, shoes worn out. Lifting me off the ground, arms and legs aching. Now this nightmare is over, now I'm in Heaven, I'm not walking the dog again.

Chloe Halliday (11)
Swalwell Primary School, Newcastle upon Tyne

Fear

Feet striding, they're getting louder and louder. Footsteps coming closer, closer. The owls hooting, the eyes observing and the ears listening. Walking through in the starless and moist night. The moonlight is nearly full. Beware of the werewolves, argh, argh!

I wish I didn't have a fear of the dark.

Ashley Turner (11)
Swalwell Primary School, Newcastle upon Tyne

Black Mamba

I keep on running from them, things that have killed my family. It makes me sweat and tremble. Striking swiftly with poison, black as the scales.

I try not to fear them but they eat people as a snack. I wish I could drive away all snakes, right now!

Adam Watson (10)
Swalwell Primary School, Newcastle upon Tyne

The Strange Place

My hands were trembling when I saw that I was on a strange planet. My brain felt hypnotised in every way. Then these terrorising robots came, trying to suck my blood. As I ran these aliens came out. 'Argh!' Then I remembered that I was on a terrifying ride.

Jade Urwin (9)
Swalwell Primary School, Newcastle upon Tyne

Sheepdog

It darted this way and that. Its black and white colour streaked the wide open countryside. It shot across to round up a stray. Then the swift sheepdog returned to his master. The calm and quick sheepdog, with its tummy warm and full, curled up by the fireside to rest.

Michael Hall (10)
Swalwell Primary School, Newcastle upon Tyne